THE SAINT ON THE
SPANISH MAIN

The Saint goes island-hopping in the sunny Caribbean.

In Bimini, he confronts a jewel smuggler, in Nassau he solves a murder mystery, in The Virgin Islands . . .

Well, you can find out for yourself what he does there and at further stop-overs in Jamaica, Puerto Rico and Haiti.

THE SAINT BOOKS

Available in Hodder Paperbacks

FOLLOW THE SAINT

THE SAINT IN THE SUN

VENDETTA FOR THE SAINT

THANKS TO THE SAINT

THE SAINT'S GETAWAY

THE SAINT STEPS IN

THE SAINT ON GUARD

CALL FOR THE SAINT

THE HAPPY HIGHWAYMAN

THE SAINT V. SCOTLAND YARD

SAINT TO THE RESCUE

SAINT ERRANT

TRUST THE SAINT

THE SAINT BIDS DIAMONDS

SAINT OVERBOARD

THE SAINT MEETS HIS MATCH

SAINT IN NEW YORK

THE SAINT GOES WEST

THE SAINT IN MIAMI

FEATURING THE SAINT

THE SAINT RETURNS

THE SAINT CLOSES THE CASE

LESLIE CHARTERIS

THE SAINT ON THE
SPANISH MAIN

HODDER PAPERBACKS

The villains in this book are entirely imaginary and bear no relation to any living person.

FIRST PUBLISHED OCTOBER 1955
THIS EDITION   1960
SECOND IMPRESSION   1970

Printed in Great Britain for Hodder Paperbacks Limited, St. Paul's House, Warwick Lane, London, E.C.4, by Cox and Wyman Ltd., London, Reading and Fakenham

ISBN 0 340 12805 4

CONTENTS

BIMINI: THE EFFETE ANGLER   7

NASSAU: THE ARROW OF GOD   41

JAMAICA: THE BLACK COMMISSAR   66

PUERTO RICO: THE UNKIND PHILANTHROPIST   111

THE VIRGIN
   ISLANDS: THE OLD TREASURE STORY   137

HAITI: THE QUESTING TYCOON   161

— BIMINI —

THE EFFETE ANGLER

IT HAS been said by certain sceptics that there are already more than enough stories of Simon Templar, and that each new one added to his saga only adds to the incredibility of the rest, because it is clearly impossible that any one man in a finite lifetime should have been able to find so many adventures.

Such persons only reveal their own failure to have grasped one of the first laws of adventure, which can only be stated quite platitudinously: Adventures happen to the adventurous.

In the beginning, of course, Simon Templar had sought for it far and wide, and luck or his destiny had lent a generous hand to the finding of it. But as the tally of his adventures added up, and the name of the Saint, as he called himself, became better known, and the legends about him were swollen by extravagant newspaper headlines and even more fantastic whisperings in the underworld, and finally his real name and likeness became familiar to inevitably widening circles, so the clues to adventure that came his way multiplied. For not only were there those in trouble who sought him out for help that the Law could not give, but there were evildoers with no fear of the Law who feared the day when some mischance might bring the Saint across their path. So that he might be anywhere, quite innocently and unsuspectingly, in a vicinity where some well-hidden wickedness was being hatched, but no guilty conscience could possibly believe that the Saint's appearance on the scene could be an accident; and therefore the ungodly, upon merely hearing his name or glimpsing a tanned piratical profile which was not hard to identify with photographs that had been published several times in eye-catching conjunction with stories not easily forgotten, would credit him with knowledge which he did not have, and would be jolted into indiscretions that they would never have committed

7

at the name of Smith or the sight of any ordinary face. In their anxiety to redouble their camouflage or to destroy him, they actually brought themselves to his attention. Thus the proliferation of his adventures tended to perpetuate itself in a kind of chain reaction. By the time of which I am now writing, he no longer had to seek adventure: it found him.

This story is as good an example as I can think of.

Don Mucklow met him in Florida at the Miami airport because they had shared more than one adventure in the Caribbean in years gone by.

"Well, what brings you here this time, Saint?"

"Nothing in particular. I just felt in the mood for some winter sunshine, so I thought I'd go island-hopping and see what cooked."

"God, you have a tough life."

Don was now married, a father, and the overworked manager of a boatyard and yacht basin.

"So it's back to the old Spanish Main again, eh?" Don said. "There must be something in that pirate tradition that you can't get away from. Which of the islands are you planning to raise hell on first?"

"I haven't even decided that yet. I may end up throwing darts at a map. Anyway, we've got to spend at least one night out on this town before I take off."

"You want to go to the Rod and Reel with me tonight?"

"What's on?"

"The usual Wednesday night dinner. And on this distinguished occasion, the presentation to Don Mucklow of his badge for catching the world's record dolphin for three-thread line, thirty-seven and a half beautiful pounds of it, even on the official certified scale."

Simon turned and beamed at him.

"Why, you cagy old son of a gun," he said affectionately. "Congratulations! How did you ever manage to stuff all those sinkers down its throat without anyone seeing you?"

"I just live right. But I certainly had my fingers crossed till the IGFA approved it."

"Now who has the tough life? What I wouldn't give to tie into a really important fish!"

"Why don't you stick around and try? I'll fix you up with a good skipper."

"Don't tempt me. What other entertainment is the Rod and Reel offering, besides the privilege of seeing Mucklow look smug, like an Eagle Scout with his new badge?"

"There's a talk by Walton Smith on some new discoveries they've made about the migration of tuna."

"That should be most educational."

"And then, just to please people like you, we're having a girl called Lorelei, who takes her clothes off in a fishbowl."

"Now you're starting to sell it," said the Saint.

So by seven o'clock that evening they were part of a convivial mob of members and guests at the bar of the exclusive Rod and Reel club on Palm Island. Don, who knew everybody, contrived to elude conversational ambushes until he had attained the prime objective of getting their first drink order filled; then, when they each had a tall Peter Dawson in hand, he reached into the milling crowd and pulled out a short, broad-shouldered man with ginger hair surrounding a bald spot like a tonsure.

"Patsy, who let you in here?"

"I was brought by a member an' a foine gentleman," said the other with dignity. "Although judgin' by yourself as a member, that might sound like two different people."

"I've a friend here who's looking for you, Patsy."

"Indade?"

"This is Captain O'Kevin," Don said to the Saint. "Patsy, meet Simon Templar."

O'Kevin shook hands with a strong bony grip. His pug-nosed face was a mosaic of freckles and red sunburn that would never blend into an even brown, out of which his faded green eyes twinkled up from a mass of creases.

"That sounds like a name I should be knowin'. Wait – this couldn't be the fellow they call the Saint?"

"That's him," Don said. "And I just hope you haven't got any skeletons in your locker."

9

"Fortunately, I earn an honest livin' instid of operatin' a thievin' boatyard." O'Kevin's bright little eyes searched Simon's face more interestedly. "Now why would the Saint be trailin' a poor hardworkin' charter-boat captain, for the Lard's sake?"

"Because he wants to go fishing," Don said. "He isn't satisfied with being the most successful buccaneer since Captain Kidd, he wants to try and take my only record away from me. So I said I'd put him on to a good skipper. Naturally I picked you, because your customers never catch anything. You can give him a nice boat ride, and I won't have a thing to worry about."

"Sure, an' 'twould be a pleasure to foind him something bigger than that overgrown mullet ye're boastin' about. How long would ye be stayin' down here, Mr Templar?"

"Not more than a day or two," said the Saint.

"That's too bad. I've a party waitin' for me in Bimini right now, an' I'm leavin' first thing in the marnin'. I'll be gone three or four days."

"What's your hurry, Simon?" Don protested. "Those islands have been out there in the Caribbean a long time. They won't run away."

"Where are ye makin' for, Mr Templar?" O'Kevin asked.

Simon grinned. Only a few hours ago he had talked about throwing darts at a map. Now a dart had been thrown for him. It was one of those utterly random choices that appealed to his gambling instinct.

"I've just this minute decided," he said. "I'm going to Bimini, too."

"Then I'll most likely run into ye over there. It's been nice meetin' ye, sorr, even though somebody should o' warned ye about the company ye're keepin'."

He shook hands again, winked amiably at Don, and was swept aside by an eddy of thirsty newcomers.

"No kidding," Don told the Saint, "Patsy's one of the best fishing captains around here."

"And you knew very well he was booked before you introduced me."

"I did not. Any more than I knew you were going to Bimini. What on earth made you suddenly decide that?"

"It was the first island I'd heard mentioned since I got here," said the Saint cheerfully. "So I let that be an omen. I had to pick one of 'em eventually, anyway. A dear old aunt of mine ruined a lot of bookies picking race horses by a similar system."

"Well, Patsy isn't the only good skipper. Let's see who else is here tonight."

They met several dozens of other men, in an accelerating kaleidoscope whose successive patterns soon overtaxed even Simon Templar's remarkable memory, in the good humoured turmoil of a typical stag party. But at the end of the meeting, after the dinner and presentation of badges and the lecture and the artistic performance of the girl called Lorelei (who, I regret to inform those readers who were only staying with us for that bit, has nothing further to do with this story), the face which had impressed itself on him most sharply perhaps only because it was the first introduction of the evening sorted itself out of the dispersing crowd and approached him again.

"I've been thinkin', Mr Templar," Patsy O'Kevin said. "So long as ye're headed for Bimini, anyhow, an' if it isn't too soon for ye, maybe ye'd like to be goin' with me tomorrow? It won't cost ye nothin', an' we could do a bit o' fishin' on the way, an' if we're lucky we'll catch one that'll make this loudmouth Mucklow wish he'd used that sardine o' his for live bait."

"Take him up on it, Simon," Don said. "You might even catch one of those pink sea serpents he sees after a week on rum and coconut water."

"That's too nice an offer to pass up, Patsy," said the Saint straightly. "Thank you. I'd love it. What time do we sail?"

So if it hadn't happened like that he would never have met Mr Clinton Uckrose. Or (to supply a new focus of sex interest) Gloria. . . .

2

Mʀ Uckrose, Simon learned on the way over, was an
American, rich and retired, living in Europe. He had
been in the jewellery manufacturing business in New York,
but had sold out to his partner, and had become a legal resident
of the principality of Monaco, by which device he escaped paying any income tax on his invested capital, since the profits
from the Monte Carlo casino absolved the happy inhabitants
of Monaco from any such depressing obligation. He was so
morbidly apprehensive about jeopardizing this delicate but
agreeable situation that nothing would induce him to set foot
in the United States again, for fear that by touching American
soil he might provide the Internal Revenue Department with
grounds for some claim against him. Although he had become
a regular winter visitor in Nassau, and liked to get in some big-
game fishing during his stay, he flew directly to the Bahamas
via London and Bermuda, and refused to take the short fifty-
minute additional flight to Miami for his sport: instead, he
took a Bahamian Airways plane to Bimini, most westerly of
the islands and only some fifty miles off the Florida coast, and
sent for a charter boat to come over and join him there. A
former business connection of Uckrose's had recommended
Patsy O'Kevin the first time, and this would make the third
consecutive year that the stocky Irishman had been booked for
the same assignment.

This had not made O'Kevin any more enthusiastic about it.

" 'Tis not that he's stingy, Simon, which I'll be so bowld as
to call ye. An' wid the competition these days, a captain should
give thanks for ivry charter he gets. But there's not a drap o'
real fisherman's blood in him." O'Kevin watched approvingly
as the Saint used a sharpened brass tube to core the spine out
of a ballyhoo, the slender little bait fish that looks so aptly like
a miniature of some of the big-billed fishes it is used to lure.
"Niver would Mr Uckrose soil his hands by puttin' thim closer
to a fish than the other end av a rod."

Simon slid the ballyhoo on to a hook and bound it with a few deft twists of leader wire. Now, when it went in the water it would troll with its limp tail fluttering exactly as if it were swimming alive.

"I'm just a free-loader," he said lightly. "If I were paying for this, I might expect service, too."

"Niver would Mr Uckrose use that rod an' six-thread line," O'Kevin persisted. "All he'll use is the heaviest tackle I've got, so that whiniver he hooks anything, so long as the hook holds, he can just harse it in. If I had a derrick an' a power winch, he'd be usin' that. An' any toime there's a little braize blowin', we'll stay right at the dock. Mr Uckrose is afraid he'll be seasick."

"That isn't his fault, Patsy."

"Thin he shouldn't be tryin' to pretend he's a fisherman," said O'Kevin arbitrarily. "For it seems all he cares about is to come in wid some fish, he doesn't care what kind it is or how it was caught, just so he can be havin' his picture taken with it, an' send it to his friends if it's eatable or have it stuffed if it isn't, so they'll think what a great spartsman he is, when there's no spart to it. An' that's the kind o' client I'd like to be rich enough to turn down." The captain spat forcefully to lee. "Now get that bait in the water, Simon, before I start thinkin' ye're a man after Uckrose's heart rather than me own!"

Simon laughed, and put the bait over the side.

O'Kevin's mate eased off the throttles as the *Colleen* knifed her trim forty-foot hull out of the green coastal water into the deep blue of the Gulf stream, a boundary almost as sharply marked as the division between a river and its bank. He was a thin, dark, intense-looking young man who never opened his mouth unless he was directly spoken to, and not always then. "We call him Des," O'Kevin said, "after the chap in those Philip Wylie stories." His air of nervous compression suggested the mute strain of a hunting dog on a leash.

When the Saint threw the brake on his reel, O'Kevin reached for the line, nipped it in a clothespin, and hauled it out to the end of one of the outriggers that had already been lowered to stand out from the boat's side like a long, sensitive antenna. With the outrigger holding it clear of the *Colleen's* wake, the ballyhoo wiggled and skipped enticingly through the tops of the waves far behind them. The Saint settled the butt of the rod securely in the socket between his thighs, leaned comfortably back in the fishing chair, and watched the trail of bait lazily with his blue eyes narrowed against the glare. Patsy opened a cold can of beer, and put it into his hand. This was the life, Simon thought, feeling the sun warm his bare back and letting his weight balance harmoniously with the gentle surge and roll of the boat, and he didn't give a damn about Mr Uckrose or any of his shortcomings.

"Now, Mrs Uckrose is diff'rent altogether," Patsy said presently, as if some obscure need for this amplification had been worrying him. "Gloria's her name, an' glorious she is to look at, though I'm thinkin' she needs a stronger hand on the tiller than Uckrose is man enough to be givin' her. If I were as young as yerself—"

"*Sail!*" shouted Des in a sudden hysterical bark.

Simon had already seen it himself, the long dorsal fin that lanced the water behind and to one side of the diving and flirting ballyhoo. It disappeared, then showed again briefly on the other side of the bait, still following it.

Suddenly the line broke out of the light grip of the clothes-pin that held it at the end of the outrigger, and the slack of it drifted astern from the Saint's rod tip.

It must perhaps be explained to those who have not yet been initiated into this form of angling that a member of the swordfish family does not attack a lure like a bass hitting a plug or a trout rising to a fly. It first strikes its intended victim with its bill, to kill or stun it: this is the blow that jerks the line from the outrigger, and with the line released the bait is for a few seconds no longer towed by the boat and drops back with convincing lifelessness, while the fish that struck it circles into position to take a comfortable gulp at the prospective snack. The precise timing of this wait is a matter of fine judgment curbing the excitement of a suspense that makes seconds seem to stretch out into minutes.

"*Now!*" howled O'Kevin; and even as he said it the Saint

had flipped the drag on his reel, and was lifting his rod tip up and back. "And again!" yelled the captain, dancing a little jig; but already the Saint was rearing back again, so that the slender rod tip bowed in a sharp curve, tightening the line strongly yet with a controlled smoothness that would not snap it. "Again! That's right! That should have hooked the spalpeen—"

A hundred and fifty yards astern the fish shot up out of the water, shaking its head furiously, the whole magnificent stream-lined length of it seeming to walk upright on its thrashing tail. The sunlight flashed on its silver belly, shone on the sleek mid-night blue of its back, stencilled the outline of the enormous spread sail of dorsal fin from which the fish took its name. Then after what seemed like an incredible period of levitation it fell back into the sea with a mighty splash. The reel under Simon's hand whined in protest as the line tore off it.

"Holy Mother of God," said O'Kevin reverently. "That's the biggest grandfather av a sailfish these owld eyes iver hope to be gladdened by the sight av. If it weighs one pound it'll weigh a hundred an' twenty. No, it's bigger'n that. It's twenty pounds bigger. It's a world record! . . . Des! Is it dreamin' ye are?" As if waking out of a trance himself, he scrambled back to the wheel, pushed his mate aside, hauled back on the clutches and gunned the engines, his gnarled hands moving with the light-ning accuracy of a concert pianist's. "Howld on, Simon me boy," he breathed. "Play him as gently as if ye had him tied to a cobweb, an' me an' the *Colleen* will do the rest!"

If this story were about nothing but fishing, the chronicler could happily devote several pages to a blow-by-blow account of the Saint's tussle with that specimen of *Istiophorus ameri-canus*; but they would be of interest mainly to fishermen. Those who have had a taste of light-tackle fishing for big-game fish know that when you have more than a hundred pounds of finny dynamite on the end of a line which is only guaranteed to support eighteen pounds of dead weight, you do not just crank the reel until you wind up your catch alongside the boat. All you can do is to apply firm and delicate pressure, keeping the line tight enough so that he cannot throw it off the hook, yet not so taut that it would snap at a sudden movement. If he decides to take off for other latitudes, you cannot stop him, you can only keep this limited strain on him and wait for him to tire. But you also have only a limited length of line on your reel for him to run with, and if he takes all of it you have lost him; so the boat must follow him quickly on every run so that he never gets too far away. In this manoeuvring the boat captain's skill is almost as vital as the fisherman's.

Patsy O'Kevin was obviously an expert captain, but on that occasion his eagerness turned his skill into a liability. He was so anxious not to let a probable record get away, so afraid of letting the Saint put too much strain on his frail line, that he followed the fish as closely as a seasoned stock horse herding a calf – so quickly and closely that the Saint had a job to keep any pressure on the fish at all. And so there were several more jumps, and many more runs, and time went on until it seemed to have lost meaning; and then at last there was a moment when the fish turned in its tracks and came towards the boat like a torpedo, the Saint reeling in frantically, and O'Kevin for once was slow, and fumbled over throwing the clutches from reverse to forward. The bellying line passed right under the transom, right through the churning of the propellers, and as the Saint mechanically went on winding a limp frayed end of nylon lifted clear of the wake.

No more than a boat's length off the starboard beam, the freed sailfish rose monstrously from the water for one last derisive pirouette.

"I did it," said O'Kevin brokenly. "There's no one to blame but me. If ye'd be kinder to me than I deserve, Simon, would ye just be cuttin' me throat before you throw me overboard to the sharks?"

"Forget it," said the Saint, wiping the sweat from his face. "I was getting tired of the whole thing, anyway."

He was amazed to see by his watch that the battle had lasted more than two and a half hours.

"An' almost all the time, that son of a whale was headin' almost due south," O'Kevin said. "We're further from Bimini now than we were whin we left Miami."

Only the taciturn mate had no comment. O'Kevin turned the

helm back to him, and a certain restrained melancholy settled over the whole party as the *Colleen* swung around and ploughed northwards again with the stream.

After a belated lunch of sandwiches and beer had had their restorative effect, however, Patsy finally stopped shaking his head and muttering to himself and stomped aft to the baitbox.

"If ye'll allow me to bend another bait to yer line, sorr," he said, "we may yet meet the great-grandfather o' that tadpole I lost for ye."

If this were really a fishing story, it would tell how the Saint presently hooked and fought and vanquished an even bigger sailfish, a leviathan that was likely to remain a world's record for all time. Unfortunately the drab requirements of veracity to which your historian is subject will not permit him this pleasure.

In fact, most of the northward troll yielded only one medium-sized barracuda. Then, with the islands of Bimini already clearly in sight, Simon hooked another sailfish; but it was quite a small one, only about fifty pounds, as they saw on its first jump. O'Kevin allowed Des to handle the boat, which he did efficiently enough, and in something less than an hour the exhausted fish was wallowing tamely alongside. O'Kevin reached down and grasped its bill with a gloved hand and lifted it out of the water, his other hand sliding down the wire leader. He looked at Simon inquiringly.

"Let it go," said the Saint. "We'll come back and catch him some day when he's grown up."

So this only shows exactly how and why it was that it was late afternoon when the *Colleen* threaded her way between the tricky reefs and shoals that guard the harbour entrance of Bimini, half a day later than she should normally have arrived, and flying from one of her raised outriggers the pennant with which a sport fisherman proclaims that a sailfish has been brought to the boat and voluntarily released.

The Commissioner was waiting to come aboard as they tied up. Acting as immigration, health, and customs officer combined, he glanced at their papers, accepted a drink and a cigarette, wished them a pleasant stay, and stepped back on the dock in less than fifteen minutes.

Simon had stayed behind in the cabin to pick up his suitcase. As he brought it out to the cockpit, O'Kevin was already on the pier talking to three people who stood there. Simon handed up his two-suiter, and as he swung himself up after it O'Kevin said: "This is the gintleman I was talkin' about. Mr Templar – Mr and Mrs Uckrose."

Mr Clinton Uckrose was a somewhat pear-shaped man of medium height, who looked about fifty-five, dressed in an immaculate white silk shirt and white shantung trousers with a gaudy necktie knotted around the waist for a belt. Under a peaked cap of native straw, his face also had a pear-shaped aspect, compounded of broad bloodhound jowls bracketing a congenitally aggrieved mouth and a pair of old-fashioned pince-nez which seemed to pull his eyes close together with their grip on his nose. He ignored the Saint's proffered hand and did not even seem to have heard his name.

"You've got a nerve!" he snarled.

Simon looked down at his hand, saw nothing obviously contaminating about it, and tried offering it to Mrs Uckrose. She took it.

Politeness required him to look into her eyes, which were interesting enough in a languorous, brown-velvet way; but it was not easy to keep his gaze from wandering too pointedly over her other attractions, which were displayed as candidly as a pair of very short shorts and bra to match could do it. From the roots of her chestnut hair to the toes of her sandalled feet she was so evenly suntanned that she looked like a golden statue; but there was nothing statuesque about the lingering softness of her handshake. She could hardly have been more than half her husband's age.

Simon understood exactly what she made Patsy O'Kevin think of. He was thinking the same way himself.

"What made you think you should take your friends joy-riding while I'm waiting for you here?" Uckrose was demanding of the captain.

"He was comin' here, anyhow," Patsy said, "so I thought it'd do no harm if he came wid me. O' course, when we got to fishin'—"

"When you got to fishing, you took the whole day instead of getting here as you were told to." Uckrose pointed up at the nearest outrigger. "And what does that flag mean?"

"It's a release flag, sorr."

"It's a release flag." Uckrose had a trick of repeating the last thing that had been said to him in a tone that made it sound as if the speaker could only have uttered it as a gratuitous affront. "What does that mean?"

"Mr Templar had a sailfish on, an' we turned it loose."

"You turned it loose." Uckrose's jowls quivered. "How many days, how many weeks, have I fished with you, year after year, and I've never yet caught a sailfish?"

"That's the luck o' the game, sorr."

"The luck of the game. But the very least you could have done was bring in the fish."

"It was Mr Templar's fish," Patsy said, with a little more emphasis on the name. "He said to break it off, so I did."

"It was only a little one," Simon put in peaceably.

"It was on my boat!" Uckrose blared. "It belonged to me. I could have sent it back to be mounted. What difference does it make who caught it?"

Simon studied him with a degree of scientific incredulity.

"Do you seriously mean," he inquired, "that you'd have had my fish stuffed, and hung over your mantelpiece, and told everyone you caught it?"

"You mind your own business!"

The Saint nodded agreeably, and turned to O'Kevin.

"I'm sorry I got you into this, Patsy," he said. "But let's just get you out again." He put a hand in his pocket, brought out some money, and peeled off two fifty-dollar bills. "That should take care of today's charter. Don't charge Fat Stuff for it, and he can't squawk. His time starts tomorrow. And thanks for the fishing – it was fun."

As O'Kevin hesitated, Simon tucked the two fifties into his shirt pocket and picked up his suitcase.

Gloria Uckrose said: "Did I get the name right – Simon Templar?"

Simon nodded, looking at her again, and this time taking no

19

pains to control where his eyes wandered. With all his audacity he was not often crudely brash; there is a difference which the cut-rate Casanovas of the Mickey Spillane school would never understand. But Clinton Uckrose's egregious rudeness had sparked an answering insolence in him that burned up into more outrageous devilment than solemn outrage.

"I'll be staying at the Compleat Angler," he said. "Any time you can shake off this dull slob, let's have a drink."

He started to walk away.

The third member of the party who had been waiting on the pier intercepted him. He had been with the Uckroses when Simon first saw them, but standing a little behind them. He had not been introduced, and during all the talk that followed he had remained a little apart. He was a slim man of about thirty in a rumpled seersucker suit, with a light panama hat shading a long blue-chinned face and heavy-lidded black eyes. Simon had observed those details at a glance, but had taken no other notice of him.

Now the man had moved so that the Saint either had to back up and make a wide detour or pass along the very edge of the dock through a space that was barely wide enough to admit him. Simon coolly kept going. The man was looking right at him and said: "Mr Uckrose don't like fresh guys."

Then he hit the Saint low in the belly with his left hand and pushed with his right.

The Saint's sinewy leanness made it deceptively easy to misjudge his weight, and his reflexes worked on hair triggers. Fantastic as it seemed in that setting, the slim man's approach had a certain standardized professional quality which had given Simon a split second's warning. The man's fist only grazed a set of abdominal muscles that were already braced to the consistency of a truck tyre, and the push with his right hand rocked the Saint, but did not send him flying off the dock as it should have. For an instant Simon was precariously off balance; and then as the other instinctively pushed again Simon ducked and twisted like a cat, and it was the slim man who incredulously found himself floating off into space to pancake on the water with a fine liquid smack.

Simon Templar looked down at him as he came spluttering to the surface, shook his head reproachfully, and sauntered on.

It was only after that that he realized intelligently what he had reacted to intuitively: that for a retired manufacturing jeweller Mr Uckrose had a champion whose technique was extraordinarily reminiscent of a gangster's bodyguard.

3

SIMON SURRENDERED his bag to one of an insistent troop of black boys, as the simplest way of getting rid of the rest, and walked thoughtfully along the one street of Bimini, which follows the shore of the lagoon. Any day now, perhaps, some ambitious commercial enterprise will descend on that little ridge of palm-topped coral and transform it into a tropical Coney Island; but at this time the street still led only from the neighbourhood of the small trim Yacht Club, near which Simon had landed, to the vicinity of the homelike Compleat Angler hotel, with a scattering of shacks in between, some of them selling liquor or groceries or souvenirs, which had a paradoxical look of having been left over from a Hollywood picture about the South Seas. The island was still nothing much more than a stopover for yachts cruising into the Bahamas, or a base for fishermen working the eastern side of the Gulf Stream.

The Saint frowned. Having started to walk away, in a rather effective exit, he could scarcely turn back and say to the slim man, or even to Uckrose, "By the way, chum, *are* you some sort of gangster?" Besides, there was still something not quite right with the picture. There were plenty of gangsters in the Miami area, which had always appealed to them for the same reasons as it appealed to any other class of wealthy vacationer; but Bimini had only attracted them during Prohibition, when cargoes of potable spirits could be assembled there under the tolerant protection of the British flag, to be loaded on to fast motorboats for a quick night run to the dry coast of the United States. Now the island offered nothing either to enrich or entertain them. Anyhow, he saw no reason to disbelieve the story that Mr Uckrose came there from Europe, not from the States. And somehow he could not exactly visualize Mr Uckrose as a gangster – not even of the modern, big-business, board of directors, crime syndicate chieftain type. Furthermore, if Uckrose had been one of those, the Saint would almost certainly have recognized him.

No; he might have to take some of it back, about the 'gangster' part. But the 'bodyguard' feature could not be laughed away – or the fact that the blue-chinned warrior certainly hadn't learned his methods in any lace-collar school.

Simon Templar took a leisurely shower, put on a clean pair of denim slacks and a shirt that could have been used to advertise an exotic flower show, and went down to the bar to buy himself a Dry Sack before dinner.

He was half way through his meal when the Uckroses and the slim droopy-eyed man came in and sat down at a corner table on the other side of the dining-room. If Simon had given more thought to it, he realized that he might have expected that: the island offered no variety of first class hotels for anyone to choose from. But in the overwhelmingly civilized atmosphere of a British hotel dining-room, even in such an unassuming outpost of the Empire, in the presence of soft-footed waiters and a handful of other conventional guests, a situation that might have been explosive seemed to be decisively dampened. Clinton Uckrose and his bodyguard glanced at him only once, and thereafter studiously ignored him. The conversation at their table was inaudible, but seemed to remain at a commonplace desultory level, and the faces of the two men were inexpressive, with the deliberate woodenness of poker players. Only Gloria kept on looking at the Saint, and seemed to be paying little attention to the talk of her companions. She had changed into a low-cut white dress that provided a striking contrast for her brown skin and dark copper hair, and which made her superlative torso even more intriguing than the bra top in which he had first seen it. He found her eyes on him again and again, and her gaze did not waver when he discovered it. A kind of secret smile lurked around her mouth and let him wonder whether it was meant for him to share or not.

He finished, and went out to the lounge, where he found the proprietor. They exchanged a couple of polite trivialities, and Simon said: "The younger of the two men at the corner table in there, with the show-stopper in white – I feel I've met him somewhere before. Do you know his name?"

The proprietor turned and picked up the register.

"Mr Vincent Innutio," he said, pointing to the entry. "From Naples. He came here with Mr and Mrs Uckrose."

"No bell." Simon shook his head. "I guess it must just be a resemblance."

Even the Saint could not know every minor malefactor on two continents, but the name sounded as if it would fit very well on some subordinate hoodlum who might have been tagged as an undesirable alien and forcibly shipped home from America to his native Italy, where Mr Uckrose could have found him and adopted him. But why Mr Uckrose would want him was still another question.

By this time, of course, the Saint knew very well that he had already reached the middle of another adventure without even having noticed the point at which it started to close around him. But he was quite happy to let it continue to enmesh him, without rushing it.

Exactly as he would have done if nothing out of the ordinary had happened, he arranged for a native guide with a skiff to take him bonefishing early the next morning, and went to bed. As his one concession to the intrinsic hazards of the situation, he wedged the back of a chair under his door knob, after assuring himself that his window was reasonably inaccessible from outside; aside from that, he relied on his ability to sleep like a watchdog to protect him. He read *Time* for an hour, turned out the light, and slept tranquilly until dawn. An hour later, fortified with bacon and eggs and coffee, he was rigging a rod loaned him by the hotel proprietor, while a cheerful displaced African ferried him down the bay.

Again this is no occasion to detail his morning's stalking of the elusive bonefish, which is esteemed to be the spookiest and at the same time the fightingest thing that swims. He was well satisfied to put two in the boat, the larger of which would scale close to six pounds. By one o'clock his eyes ached from searching the brilliant water, he was hot and thirsty and getting hungry again, and most of the mud flats were high and dry; he was glad to agree with the boatman that they should knock off until the turn of the tide.

As the boy started to row back across the lagoon, Simon saw the *Colleen* coming through the inlet, riding high on her step with a creaming wave at her bow. In a few minutes she was snug at her berth, and almost at once three figures were walking away from her along the pier. Even at that distance the Saint's keen eyes could identify them by their silhouettes, and he told his boatman to change course towards the *Colleen* with the assurance that the Uckroses and Vincent Innutio would be well out of the way by the time he got there.

Patsy O'Kevin passed Des the hose with which he had been helping his mate to swab down, and gave Simon a hand over the side with a big grin.

"Faith, 'tis a proud man I am to be shakin' the hand that pushed that spaghetti merchant into the drink. An' if only it'd pushed Uckrose in after him, I'd be kissin' it. As it is, ye can ask me for anything except the *Colleen* herself."

"How about a cold beer?" Simon suggested.

With the cool nectar freshening his mouth and throat, he said: "You hadn't warned me about Innutio. Where does he fit on?"

"I niver met him before, ayther. Uckrose calls him his secretary, but by the cut av his jib I'd say he'd be handier wid the kind o' typewriter that only prints three letters, RIP. As ye saw for yerself!"

Simon nodded.

"Why would Uckrose need that kind of bodyguard?"

"I couldn't be guessin'. Although 'tis likely enough he'd always be givin' someone the notion to be takin' a poke at him. Now that ye've seen him in action, there's no more I can tell ye."

"He is really retired, is he? Or has he ever said anything about still dabbling in business?"

"According to him, the only jewellery he iver wants to see again is what he can hang on his wife."

"That's nice hanging, now you mention it. And the stuff I saw her wearing last night wasn't coloured glass."

"Maybe he thinks he needs the wop to take care av it."

"Insurance would cost a lot less, unless she's going around with a maharani's collection."

"Maybe he can't get insurance," O'Kevin said.

Simon took another prolonged swallow of beer. He was feeling better all the time.

"What brought you back so early today?" he asked.

"It was like a mill pond when we set out, which was foine, an' Uckrose caught a dolphin, about twelve pounds. Thin it started blowin' just enough to ruffle the water, so pretty soon he says he's got a headache an' he wants to go in – the way I told you it always is." Patsy opened the fishbox aft and held up the dolphin. "But just in case we niver catch anything else, I'm to keep this frozen, an' this hardly enough for a good dinner, an' if it should be all he catches he'll send it back to Miami to be stuffed." He dropped the fish back on the ice and slammed the lid of the box disgustedly. "Would ye have a little appetite left, Simon? I got some conch last night an' brewed a foine pot o' chowder for the Uckroses lunch, but His Lardship wouldn't eat while we were out, an' it's just goin' to waste."

"We can't let it do that," said the Saint.

It was good chowder, rich and creamy, with plenty of chewy conch meat in it.

"If Uckrose had et some av it he might o' made Gloria a lot happier," O'Kevin said as he finished his bowl.

There is a widespread belief in those parts that the flesh of that giant species of marine snail possesses aphrodisiac properties far exceeding those of the traditionally respected oyster, which was doubtless what O'Kevin was alluding to. His thoughts seemed to continue along that track, for he went on as if it were in the most natural sequence: "If ye don't give her the benefit av it yourself, ye're not the man I've heard tell ye are."

"What makes you think she'd be so amenable?" Simon asked amusedly.

"Because she's gettin' thoroughly tired of Uckrose, as anyone can see. Already today she's sayin' how bored she is wid his way o' fishin'. But he won't hear o' me takin' her out alone if it's too rough for him. So she tells him she's a mind to go right back to Nassau where she could do things an' have fun. She's as ripe and ready for trouble as a woman ever will be, Simon me b'y, an' if ye don't take advantage av it it's a disillusioned owld man I'll be."

Simon accepted a cigarette and a cup of coffee, and then headed back to the hotel. By that time the cumulative effect of the food and beer on top of the long sun-drenched morning was making the ancient tropical custom of a siesta seem remarkably intelligent and inviting. He took a cold shower, closed the jalousie shutters enough to produce a restful twilight, and stretched out naked on the bed to relax and think.

Somewhere nearby, some aspiring native Crosby with a guitar was rehearsing an apocryphal calypso:

> *Oh, le' we go down to Bimini –*
> *You never get a lickin' till you go down to Bimini . . .*

Simon wondered idly what historic rhubarb was commemorated in that quaint refrain.

> *Bimini gal is a rock in de harbour –*
> *You never git a lickin' till you go down to Bimini!*

And that also could provide sustenance for extensive speculation.

Ta-tap . . . ta-ta-tap!

The knocks were on his door, very softly yet quite distinctly. In a flash he was on his feet, pulling on his trousers and zipping them up. But as the knocks were repeated, even through their stealthiness he detected a certain flippancy in their odd little rhythm, a kind of conspiratorial gaiety that was persuasively reassuring. It would have taken an almost incredible Machiavelli of an assassin to have put that subtle touch into a knock. Simon was practically sure of what he would see as he turned the door knob.

26

Gloria Uckrose came in, wearing a green silk dressing-gown and apparently nothing else.

4

"I THOUGHT," she said, "I'd see whether you were kidding, about joining you for a drink."

"Throw on a dress," said the Saint agreeably, "and I'll be waiting for you in the bar."

"I'd be more comfortable here."

"Then I'd have to get you something."

"I don't really need anything. I'll settle for just joining." She had come all the way into the room, walking confidently across towards the window. Now she stood with a cigarette in a short holder in her mouth, her velvet eyes resting on him a little mockingly through the trickle of smoke. "Why don't you shut the door?"

Simon leaned on the handle, fanning the door a little wider if anything.

"Your husband mightn't understand," he explained ingeniously. "He might follow you here, and come bursting in brandishing a revolver. He might even be acquitted if he shot me."

She laughed shortly.

"My husband would be too scared of the bang to pull the trigger. Anyway, he's snoring his head off. He had three double Daiquiris before lunch, and I know exactly what they do to him. A hurricane wouldn't wake him up before cocktail time."

"Which room do you have?"

"The third door along to your left. Why?"

"Would you think me unduly nervous if I went and listened to this snore myself?"

"Not at all. Go ahead."

"In that case I don't need to," said the Saint cryptically. He started to shut the door, stopped again, and said: "What about Brother Innutio? Suppose he notices something that he thinks Clinton should hear about?"

27

"He took dramamine on the boat. He could hardly keep his eyes open through lunch."

Simon closed the door.

"It's nice to meet someone as wide awake as you," he murmured. "You probably even know already exactly what you'd say if Clinton happened to catch you coming back into the room in that costume."

"This?" The careless gesture she made bared a few more inches of brown thigh in the opening of her robe. "Of course. I wanted some ice water, and nobody answered the bell, so I went looking for someone."

"It's a bore having to think of all these things, isn't it?" he said disarmingly.

"You sound rather like a man who's had the badger game tried on him."

"I have," Simon admitted. "It's never worked, though."

"Don't even pretend to apologize. I expected you to be careful – I'd have been disappointed if you weren't. We don't have to play games, Saint. I know who you are."

He dipped into a pack of cigarettes on the bedside table and placed one in his mouth. It was like driving an unfamiliar road full of potholes and blind curves, improvising a serpentine course from instant to instant between the minor pitfalls, while never knowing what major trap might yawn around the next bend. But his hand was light and flexible on the steering, his blue eyes relaxed and receptive for all their vigilance.

"I had a feeling you connected with the name," he said. "Even if your gentlemen companions didn't."

"Those idiots!" she said contemptuously. "They were so busy with their own yapping, they wouldn't have heard your name if it had been J. Edgar Hoover."

"Brother Innutio at least acted as if he should have recognized that one. Hoover, I mean."

"I think Vince has just seen too many gangster movies."

"Are you trying to tell me that that's been his only contact?"

She shrugged.

"How should I know? He was recommended by a New York

28

detective agency. Anyway, Clinton encourages the act. It makes him feel big, or something."

Perfectly normal, just a common idiosyncrasy.

"And what's Clinton's excuse for needing a bodyguard at all?" Simon inquired conversationally.

She stared at him blankly.

"You mean you don't know?"

"I haven't the remotest idea."

Although he could lie brilliantly when the occasion called for it, the truth could be told with a pellucid simplicity that it would have been almost impossible to give to a falsehood. The incredulous widening of her eyes was merely automatic: his honesty was so obvious that it would have convinced anyone. But for the moment the fact as he stated it left her speechless.

"So that's how it is," she said at last. "I've got to face it now."

"Face what?" he asked politely.

She sat down on the arm of the chair nearest to her, careless of how the robe fell off her legs.

"What I've been dreading for a long time," she said. "He's losing his mind. I thought he was a little touched when he hired Vincent. But he swore that people were following him and spying on him. He talked about being kidnapped or murdered for something he'd known about before he retired. And when you arrived here, and it finally dawned on him who you were, he was sure that you were working for these people and you'd only come here to get him."

"His captain could have told him that we met entirely by accident, and all I ever knew about your husband until I got here was what Patsy told me."

"I know. Captain O'Kevin told him that. But he wouldn't believe it. He's certain that you knew Captain O'Kevin would be at the Rod and Reel Club, and you planned to meet him there to make it easier for you to get close to us when you got here."

Simon lowered himself on to the bed and leaned back against the headboard, hitching one leg up to rest an arm on his knee.

"And who are the sinister mob that's supposed to be behind that elaborate piece of delirium?"

"I don't know. He's never discussed any of his business with me. And when I tried to ask him about this thing in particular, he told me it was better for me not to know. But he almost had me believing in it until a minute ago."

"Was I the only real test? You'd never seen any other suspicious characters lurking around, with your own eyes? Nobody ever had tried to actually do anything to him?"

"Not that I ever saw."

The Saint slowly and carefully created a perfectly formed smoke ring.

"Then it certainly does look as if your husband is at least mildly squirrelly," he said. "If it's any comfort to you, I can give you my word that I had no designs on him whatsoever when I met Patsy."

"It doesn't matter now." She stirred with a sudden restlessness. "I was going to have to get away from him somehow. You can't go on looking at a man twenty times a day and wondering how blind you can have been to marry him. I already told him I'm taking the plane back to Nassau tomorrow. The only difference now is that this'll probably be for keeps. Maybe it's not very noble of me, but I don't want to be around when his delusions get worse. How do I know when he might start suspecting *me*?"

"I can see how that might make you uncomfortable," said the Saint, with an absolutely straight face.

"I'm even more glad I came to see you."

"Parden my curiosity," he said, "but if Clinton had you half believing in his hallucinations, especially after I showed up – why *did* you come to see me?"

"You invited me, didn't you?"

"Yes."

"And right there on the dock, you knew I wanted to accept."

"But suppose I'd told you, yes, I really did have something unpleasant in mind for your husband? What did you figure on doing then?"

"I was going to offer to help you."

30

In his position, Simon was cushioned against falling down; but he lounged a little more limply, and he was glad that he had no need to pretend that he was completely unsurprised.

"That was certainly very friendly," he remarked, with prodigious moderation.

She stood up, and again her dark eyes had the same veiled amusement that they had held when she first came in.

"I'm sure it isn't the first time that a woman's wanted to team up with you."

"Well, no," he said.

She picked the remaining third of her cigarette out of the holder and held it up for a moment.

"You see? No lipstick. No incriminating evidence." She stubbed the butt out in an ashtray and dropped the holder into the pocket of her robe. "I could be useful. I'm very competent. I think of things."

"I'd noticed that."

She came closer to the bed, near enough for him to have touched her if he moved a little.

"I suppose I should be coy," she said. "But my time's so short. I'm sure you know what kind of husband I've had all these years. I need a man. Don't you want to make love to me?"

It had been coming to that ever since she knocked on his door, and he had always known it, but it had seldom been said to him so forthrightly. He met her unwavering gaze with a tinge of utterly immoral admiration, before his eyes were involuntarily drawn down to the valley where the green robe had fallen open to her waist.

"Yes, they're real," she said.

She made an almost imperceptible supple movement, and the robe slipped off her shoulders and down to her elbows.

He would always remember it as one of the most fabulous feats of self-control in his life that kept him looking at her without moving.

"Don't you at least think you should lock the door?" he asked steadily.

"Yes. No. Oh, I'm a fool!" She twitched the robe over her shoulders again, wrapping it tightly around her. "But you're so right. And you do things so gracefully. Of course it's impossible here. We've got to get away first, where we won't have to feel tense. Will you come to Nassau?"

"With you, tomorrow?"

"No, that'd be too obvious, wouldn't it? Clinton would be sure to make a scene, and either he wouldn't let me go or he'd suddenly decide to come, too." She ran a hand through her burnished hair. "And you mustn't stay here after I've gone. You'd have real trouble with Vince – you would have already, only I talked them out of it. Oh, I know you can take care of yourself, but there are so many ways to stab a man in the back, and I won't risk that when I've only just found you, before we've even . . . Wait, I've got it! There must be a charter plane service in Miami."

"There's one on the MacArthur Causeway that flies small planes over here."

"You could phone over and get one here in an hour."

"Probably. And I announce that I'm going back to Miami, but after I've taken off I hand the pilot some more green stuff and tell him I've changed my mind and I want to be flown to Nassau."

"And I'll be there with you tomorrow. Please, Simon, will you?"

He tried to keep his eyes level, but there was a reckless glint in them that would not be smothered altogether.

"What about you, Gloria?"

"If I let you down," she vowed, "you can take any Saintly revenge you can think of."

Simon Templar grinned.

"You've got a deal, darling."

She leaned over to mould her mouth against his, ignoring the looseness of the green robe. This time he could not keep quite still.

5

AND SO the shadows of the spindly coconut palms were growing longer and cooler as the Saint strolled westwards along
the lazy curve of Bimini's one uncongested street.

The radiophone contact with Miami had been surprisingly
fast and adequate. The charter plane service had been willing
and competently businesslike. For Simon Templar to pack up
for a weekend or a trip around the world was practically
the same operation, and he had done it so often that he could
complete it in a matter of minutes without even being conscious of an interruption in whatever train of thought he was
pursuing. He had plenty of time left to amble up to the *Colleen*
and make an absolutely essential adieu.

He thumped on the deck with a bottle which he had pur-
chased on the way; and Patsy O'Kevin came out into the cockpit blinking a little, like a groundhog prematurely disturbed
from hibernation.

"Why, 'tis yerself again," observed the captain superfluously.
Then he got the bottle in good focus and went on with ex-
panding cordiality: "An' welcome as the tonic I think I'm
seein' there in yer hand."

He disappeared again for what seemed like a fraction of a
second, and reappeared providently armed with a couple of
glasses.

"It's only Peter Dawson," said the Saint, removing the cap
from the bottle. "They seem to be fresh out of Irish whisky
today. Will you condescend to rinse out your gullet with
Scotch?"

"So long as it's good Gaelic liquor, I'll not be complainin'."
O'Kevin kept his glass held out, as if by instinct, until only a
miracle of surface tension kept the bulging contents from running over the rim; but his bright green eyes clung shrewdly
and inquisitively to the Saint's face. "An' whatever it is ye're
celebratin', Simon, 'tis happy I am to celebrate wid ye."

The Saint filled the second glass, and looked around.

"Where's Des?" he asked.

"He got talkin' to Mike Lerner this afternoon – ye ought to meet him yerself, the great fisherman who lives here. I guess Mike must o' liked the mettle av him, for he took the lad off to see his aquarium an' the laboratory which he built for the University o' Miami, an' if I'm not lucky Mike will be givin' him a job an' I'll be lookin' for a new mate next month."

"I'm glad to hear that," Simon said, and most sincerely meant it.

"Des is a good lad," O'Kevin said grudgingly. "But not to be mentioned in the same toast wid yerself. Which, by yer leave, I shall now drink to ye."

He raised his glass, emptied two-thirds of it, wiped his lips on the back of his hand, and exhaled a rich aromatic sigh.

"An' now," he persisted remorselessly, "tell me what it is that ye're drinkin' to."

"This, Patsy, is a farewell drink."

"Where are ye goin'?"

"Away."

"Widout ever gettin' to know Gloria?"

"No. Not quite without that."

O'Kevin squinted at him.

"It was just like I towld ye, wasn't it, Simon me b'y?"

"I wouldn't call her a rock in the harbour," said the Saint.

O'Kevin chuckled and slapped his leg.

"Faith, an' it does me heart good to see that look in yer eye! Would ye be tellin' me just a little more, which it should be me roight to know as the godfather av it?"

Simon lighted a cigarette and gave a comprehensive account of his interrupted siesta. That is, except for the physical details about which chivalry and good taste imposed a gentlemanly reticence which may have been quite exasperating to his audience. But he gave a very careful and methodical account of the conversation, as much to clarify his own recollection as anything.

"So tomorrow ye'll be with her again in Nassau," O'Kevin said wistfully, holding out his glass for a refill.

"No," said the Saint.

The captain frowned.

"Maybe ye're roight, an' I shouldn't be havin' another drop, at that," he said. "It sounded to me exactly as if ye said No."

"I did." Simon poured again hospitably, and put down the bottle. "You see, she hasn't any intention of going there. The job was very delicately handled – first to establish that she was going to Nassau anyhow, then to get me interested and you might even say excited, then to dampen me down again with nervous misgivings about the obvious risks of having an affair with her then and there. I cued her a bit with that last switch, but she could easily have done it without my help if she'd had to. Then she had to put over the argument for my leaving at once, and without her. That was fairly easy, too, and I helped her again, being a kind soul under my gruff exterior."

"Ye're imaginin' things, Simon. Her arguments were only good sense."

"Of course. They had to be. I told you it was beautifully worked out. Even to the idea of my leaving ahead of her. Because if she'd left first, as a decoy, there'd always be the risk that I mightn't follow, and then she wouldn't be around to freshen the proposition. That gorgeous body of hers was always worth betting on. And if I'd been really tiresome, and refused to be coaxed the way they wanted at all, I could still be man-oeuvred into bed, or near enough to it to stage a suitable tableau for Uckrose to come busting in on, with Innutio or maybe someone else for a witness, and start pumping lead like a properly indignant husband."

"If that was the idea, Simon, ye'd be lyin' dead in yer room already."

"No, because then they'd have all the fuss and bother of a trial, and a British court might give Uckrose a lot of trouble, no matter how much provocation he could prove. It was much smarter to try to get me out of the way peacefully first, if it could be done. But don't think I didn't have goose-pimples a few times, wondering if they were as smart as I wanted them to be."

"But ye'd towld her ye had nothin' against Uckrose, ex-ceptin' perhaps his bad manners, so whoy would he be wantin' to harm ye?"

"For fear of what I might find out, Patsy. It's funny how scared some people get about that when they hear my name."

"But ye don't honestly know of anything wrong that he's doin'?"

Simon sipped his drink.

"Not specifically; not at this instant. But I do know that there is something to know. All the effort and ingenuity that's been put into trying to bamboozle me is the proof that there's something for me to look for. Isn't it silly how panic and a guilty conscience will make people put a rope around their own necks? If I'd only been left alone I'd probably never have suspected anything."

O'Kevin shook his head baffledly.

"Whoy should Uckrose be hidin' anything at all?" he objected. "Whin ye towld Gloria ye weren't after him, she towld ye herself it only proved he was crazy, as she'd been afraid he was."

"An ordinary crackpot with delusions of persecution doesn't hire a bodyguard of Innutio's type. That was her clumsiest lie, when she said that he came through a New York detective agency. Licensed agencies just don't supply characters of that kind. Innutio is a standard-brand second-string hoodlum, and Uckrose must know it: therefore Uckrose is up to no good. It's as simple as that. Gloria came to find out exactly how much I knew; and whatever that might have been I'm sure she had a plan already worked out for coping with it, using her natural equipment, which is very persuasive indeed. When I convinced her that I had no idea what Clinton is worried about, it may have shaken her even more than if I'd known everything, but there was a prearranged plan for that situation, too. . . . What will always intrigue me is who is really the brains of the act. Gloria is a great performer, but does she write her own material? Or do we underrate Brother Uckrose?"

"Simon, me b'y, if it wasn't for all those tales I've heard about ye I'd be thinkin' ye had the same delusions as Uckrose! Is it sensible now to be creditin' him wid all kinds o' wickedness whin it's more loikely he's just a little soft in the head?"

The Saint finished the modest measure of Peter Dawson

which was all he had allowed himself, and set down the glass.

"What I've been telling you is only the end of it, Patsy," he said. "The tip-off really started way back in Miami."

O'Kevin's brow wrinkled with an effort of concentration.

"Begorra, 'tis soundin' more like a detective story ivery blessed minute ye are. Beggin' yer pardon for one second, I left a pot on the stove which could be b'ilin' over while I sit here."

He got up and ducked down the companion to the saloon.

Without an instant's hesitation, and moving with the silence of a hunting leopard, the Saint followed him.

O'Kevin turned from one of the bunk settees with an automatic that he had snatched from under the pillow in his grip, but he was not expecting to find the Saint only a foot away from him. His jaw fell slackly for a split second of a pardonable paralysis, and during that interval the Saint hit it with a nicely calculated uppercut, not too light, but not too obliterative. The captain dropped quietly on the bunk.

Simon picked up the gun and tossed it out through an open porthole. Then he pulled a roll of adhesive tape from his pocket, and swiftly and expertly taped O'Kevin's wrists together behind his back, secured his ankles in the same way, and rolled him over and bent him at the knees before using several thicknesses of the remaining tape to link the wrist and ankle bindings together. The jolt with which he had lifted the captain's chin had been so well measured that O'Kevin's eyes were opening again as the Saint finished.

"On the subject of lies," said the Saint genially, "you'd so obviously been taking a nap when I came aboard that I couldn't believe you had any pot cooking. Not that I blame you for the try."

The reply which O'Kevin started to make was so manifestly irrelevant, and so offensive to the Saint's refined ears, that Simon was obliged to use the rest of the tape to seal up O'Kevin's mouth without further delay.

"I'm afraid it was you who made the first mistake, Patsy," he said. "When Don Mucklow introduced us and said I was looking for you, your guilty conscience couldn't swallow that as a figure of speech. After that, all the talk about fishing only

37

sounded like a cover-up. And when I said I was headed for Bimini, all you could think of was that I must be on the trail of this racket you're in."

He lighted a cigarette and enjoyed a leisurely inhalation.

"You pounded your brains during the evening, and decided that the really smart move, if I was as close on the trail as that, was to keep me even closer. At least that might make it easier to keep track of me; and the more you could make me think I was fooling you, the better you might be able to fool me. Besides, you still had the selfish personal angle that if I didn't know too much already, you might go on selling the idea that you weren't really connected with Uckrose except in the most innocent and professional way, which is how the operation is set up anyhow. So if it came to a blow-up, you might yet save your own skin."

He leaned against the galley bulkhead and flipped ashes fastidiously into the sink.

"Of course you didn't give yourself away by inviting me to come over with you. I didn't begin to smell the rat until you started on the tirade against Uckrose. You had a good idea there, but you overdid it. It just didn't ring quite true that you should be so bitter about a rich slob who only gave you a nice bit of business every year, even if he was a bum sportsman. It started me wondering what else there could be behind your attitude. And then, when we got here, you were alone with him just long enough to have tipped him off to the build-up you'd given me, and he had to carry on with the gag. Only he overdid it, too. I just couldn't see a successful retired business man being quite such an uninhibited boor. . . . I didn't see all this in a flash, but it filtered through gradually. And I even began to see what was developing ahead when you started the special advance work for Gloria – almost pimping for her, if I may be so rude."

O'Kevin glared up at him with his head twisted sideways, mutely, having little choice about doing it in any other way; but the Saint was quite content to conduct a monologue.

"Now the only question is, what is the racket?" he said. "Of course, I could probably get you to tell me by sticking toothpicks under your toenails, or something old-fashioned like that, but it's more fun to make it an intellectual exercise. So I shall try first to do it in my head. Listen carefully, Patsy, because you may have to explain to the others how I did it without any help from you."

He paused a moment for a final review of his thoughts, because he would always be proud of this feat of virtuosity if he brought it off.

"It has to involve some form of merchandise, because nothing else could pay off through Bimini. It must be very valuable to account for the guard and for all the concern about it. It should be something that a man could bring here from Europe, which he could land with in Nassau without any trouble, because the Customs there never bother with the baggage of American tourists. And then it only has to be put on board a charter boat working out of Miami, which would only get a perfunctory going-over by the Customs there if it was just coming back from Bimini. The two most compact and likely possibilities are narcotics and jewellery. Unless Uckrose has invented himself a completely phony background, which is less probable, the odds point to jewels."

He took a last drag at his cigarette and flicked it through the porthole.

"Then where are these jewels? Not at the hotel, because Clinton and Gloria and Vincent all went out with you this morning, and they'd never have risked me burgling their rooms or even the hotel safe while they were away if there'd been anything there to find. But all kinds of work has been done to take suspicion off the *Colleen* – and you. Des is so obviously innocent that he's an extra asset to the camouflage. So this boat should be the safest place in sight. And exactly where on the boat, if I'm to find them without taking her apart?"

O'Kevin seemed to lie even more motionless than his bonds required, as if frozen by an almost superstitious fascination. And the Saint smiled at him like a benevolent swami.

"Well, I remember something you mentioned more than once when you were knocking Uckrose, about how you'd have to take his fish back with you – any kind of fish. It seems like too fanciful a touch for you to have invented. Therefore you knew it was really going to happen, and you were trying to prepare me for it so that I wouldn't be too struck by it when it did. So I am now going to bet my roll on that very fishy story."

He went back out to the cockpit and opened the fishbox. The dolphin that O'Kevin had shown him earlier still lay there on the ice. Simon squeezed its belly hard with one hand, and knew in a moment of exquisite and unforgettable elation that he had been right, all the way to this climax. It was like having forecast a chess game up to the checkmate after the first half dozen moves.

Straight ahead of him over the transom the sun was setting, and the silhouette of a seaplane coming head-on was etched against a crimson-tinted cloud. Already he could hear the faint hum of its engine like a distant bumblebee.

With the bait-knife Simon Templar performed a deft Caesarian section that delivered the fish of a transparent plastic bag in which many hard angular objects thinly wrapped in tissue paper could be easily felt. He returned to the saloon and showed it to O'Kevin.

"I must check on Clinton's ex-partner in New York in a couple of years," he remarked. "I assume he's the receiving end of the line, and by that time they may have organized some other channel that I can hijack. But I'm afraid you'll have to go back to legitimate fishing, Patsy me b'y."

He rinsed the plastic bag under the pump and dried it on a dish towel before he put it away in his pocket. The examination of its contents could afford to wait, but his plane was already coming down for its landing on the lagoon with a roar and a rush of wind overhead.

"I wish you'd give Gloria a message," said the Saint. "Tell her she didn't really leave me cold, but I couldn't take everything else she offered and these jewels, too. On the other hand, I mightn't have been doing this at all if she hadn't tried to take me like a yokel and stand me up. There has to be some self-respect among thieves."

He went out and jumped up on to the dock and walked briskly away, wondering what he was going to write to Don Mucklow.

— NASSAU —

THE ARROW OF GOD

ONE OF Simon Templar's stock criticisms of the classic type of detective story is that the victim of the murder, the reluctant spark-plug of all the entertaining mystery and strife, is usually a mere nonentity who wanders vaguely through the first few pages with the sole purpose of becoming a convenient body in the library by the end of Chapter One. But what his own feelings and problems may have been, the personality which has to provide so many people with adequate motives for desiring him to drop dead, is largely a matter of hearsay, retrospectively brought out in the conventional process of drawing attention to one suspect after another.

"You could almost," Simon has said, "call him a *corpus derelicti*. . . . Actually, the physical murder should only be the mid-point of the story: the things that led up to it are at least as interesting as the mechanical solution of 'who done it?' . . . Personally, I've killed very few people that I didn't know plenty about first."

Coming from a man who is generally regarded as almost a detective-story character himself, this comment is at least worth recording for reference; but it certainly did not apply to the shuffling off of Mr Floyd Vosper, which caused a brief commotion on the island of New Providence in the early spring of that year.

2

WHY SIMON TEMPLAR should have been in Nassau (which, for the benefit of the untravelled, is the city of New Providence, which is an island in the Bahamas) at the time is one of those questions which always arise in stories about him, and which can only be answered by repeating that he liked to travel and was just as likely to show up there as in Nova Zembla or Namaqualand. As for why he should have been invited to the house of Mrs Herbert H. Wexall, that is another irrelevancy which is hardly covered by the fact that he could just as well have shown up at the house of Joe Wallenski (of the arsonist Wallenskis) or the White House – he had friends in many places, legitimate and otherwise. But Mrs Wexall had some international renown as a lion hunter, even if her stalking had been confined to the variety which roars loudest in plush drawing-rooms; and it was not to be expected that the advent of such a creature as Simon Templar would have escaped the attention of her salon safari.

Thus one noontime Simon found himself strolling up the driveway and into what little was left of the life of Floyd Vosper. Naturally he did not know this at the time; nor did he know Floyd Vosper, except by name. In this he was no different from at least fifty million other people in that hemisphere; for Floyd Vosper was not only one of the most widely syndicated pundits of the day, but his books (*Feet of Clay, As I Saw Them,* and *The Twenty Worst Men in the World*) had all been the selections of one book club or another and still sold by the million in reprints. For Mr Vosper specialized in the ever-popular sport of shattering reputations. In his journalistic years he had met, and apparently had unique opportunities to study, practically every great name in the national and international scene, and could unerringly remember everything in their biographies that they would prefer forgotten, and could impale and epitomize all their weaknesses with devastatingly pinpoint precision, leaving them naked and squirming on the operating table of his vocabulary. But what this merciless professional iconoclast was like as a person Simon had never heard or bothered much to wonder about.

So the first impression that Vosper made on him was a voice, a still unidentified voice, a dry and deliberate and peculiarly needling voice, which came from behind a bank of riotous hibiscus and oleander.

"My dear Janet," it said, "you must not let your innocent

42

admiration for Reggie's bulging biceps colour your estimate of his perspicacity in world affairs. The title of All-American, I hate to disillusion you, has no reference to statesmanship."

There was a rather strained laugh that must have come from Reggie, and a girl's clear young voice said: "That isn't fair, Mr Vosper. Reggie doesn't pretend to be a genius, but he's bright enough to have a wonderful job waiting for him on Wall Street."

"I don't doubt that he will make an excellent contact man for the more stupid clients," conceded the voice with the measured nasal gripe. "And I'm sure that his education can cope with the simple arithmetic of the Stock Exchange, just as I'm sure it can grasp the basic figures of your father's Dun and Bradstreet. This should not dazzle you with his brilliance, any more than it should make you believe that you have some spiritual fascination that lured him to your feet."

At this point Simon rounded a curve in the driveway and caught his first sight of the speakers, all of whom looked up at him with reserved curiosity and two-thirds of them with a certain hint of relief.

There was no difficulty in assigning them to their lines – the young red-headed giant with the pleasantly rugged face and the slim, pretty blonde girl, who sat at a wrought-iron table on the terrace in front of the house with a broken deck of cards in front of them which established an interrupted game of gin rummy, and the thin stringy man reclining in a long cane chair with a cigarette holder in one hand and a highball glass in the other.

Simon smiled and said: "Hello. This is Mrs Wexall's house, is it?"

The girl said "Yes," and he said: "My name's Templar, and I was invited here."

The girl jumped up and said: "Oh, yes. Lucy told me. I'm her sister, Janet Blaise. This is my fiancé, Reg Herrick. And Mr Vosper."

Simon shook hands with the two men, and Janet said: "I think Lucy's on the beach. I'll take you around."

Vosper unwound his bony length from the long chair,

43

looking like a slightly dissolute and acidulated mahatma in his white shorts and burnt chocolate tan.

"Let me do it," he said. "I'm sure you two ingénues would rather be alone together. And I need another drink."

He led the way, not into the house, but around it, by a flagged path which struck off to the side and meandered through a bower of scarlet poinciana. A breeze rustled in the leaves and mixed flower scents with the sweetness of the sea. Vosper smoothed down his sparse grey hair; and Simon was aware that the man's beady eyes and sharp thin nose were cocked towards him with brash speculation, as if he were already measuring another target for his tongue.

"Templar," he said. "Of course, you must be the Saint – the fellow they call the Robin Hood of modern crime."

"I see you read the right papers," said the Saint pleasantly.

"I read all the papers," Vosper said, "in order to keep in touch with the vagaries of vulgar taste. I've often wondered why the Robin Hood legend should have so much romantic appeal. Robin Hood, as I understand it, was a bandit who indulged in some well-publicized charity – but not, as I recall, at the expense of his own stomach. A good many unscrupulous promoters have also become generous – and with as much shrewd publicity – when their ill-gotten gains exceeded their personal spending capacity, but I don't remember that they succeeded in being glamorized for it."

"There may be some difference," Simon suggested, "in who was robbed to provide the surplus spoils."

"Then," Vosper said challengingly, "you consider yourself an infallible judge of who should be penalized and who should be rewarded."

"Oh, no," said the Saint modestly. "Not at all. No more, I'm sure, than you would call yourself the infallible judge of all the people that you dissect so definitively in print."

He felt the other's probing glance stab him suspiciously and almost with puzzled incredulity, as if Vosper couldn't quite accept the idea that anyone had actually dared to cross swords with him, and moreover might have scored at least even on the riposte – or if it had happened at all, that it had been anything

44

but a semantic accident. But the Saint's easily inscrutable poise gave no clue to the answer at all; and before anything further could develop there was a paragraphic distraction.

This took the form of a man seated on top of a truncated column which for reasons best known to the architect had been incorporated into the design of a wall which curved out from the house to encircle a portion of the shore like a possessive arm. The man had long curly hair that fell to his shoulders, which with his delicate ascetic features would have made him look more like a woman if it had not been complemented with an equally curly and silken beard. He sat cross-legged and upright, his hands folded symmetrically in his lap, staring straight out into the blue sky a little above the horizon, so motionless and almost rigid that he might easily have been taken for a tinted statue except for the fluttering of the long flowing white robe he wore.

After rolling with the first reasonable shock of the apparition, Simon would have passed on politely without comment, but the opportunity was irresistible for Vosper to display his virtuosity again, and perhaps also to recover from his momentary confusion.

"That fugitive from a Turkish bath," Vosper said in the manner of a tired guide to a geek show, "calls himself Astron. He's a nature boy from the Dardanelles who just concluded a very successful season in Hollywood. He wears a beard to cover a receding chin, and long hair to cover a hole in the head. He purifies his soul with a diet of boiled grass and prune juice. Whenever his diet lets him off the pot, he meditates. After he was brought to the attention of the Western world by some engineers of the Anglo-Mongolian Oil Company, whom he cured of stomach ulcers by persuading them not to spike their ration of sacramental wine with rubbing alcohol, he began to meditate about the evils of earthly riches."

"Another member of our club?" Simon prompted innocuously.

"Astron maintains," Vosper said, leaning against the pillar and giving out as oracularly as if the object of his dissertation were not sitting on it at all, "that the only way for the holders of worldly wealth to purify themselves is to get rid of as much of it as they can spare. Being himself so pure that it hurts, he is unselfishly ready to become the custodian of as much corrupting cabbage as they would like to get rid of. Of course, he would have no part of it himself, but he will take the responsibility of parking it in a shrine in the Sea of Marmora which he plans to build as soon as there is enough kraut in the kitty."

The figure on the column finally moved. Without any waste motion, it simply expanded its crossed legs like a lazy tongs until it towered at its full height over them.

"You have heard the blasphemer," it said. "But I say to you that his words are dust in the wind, as he himself is dust among the stars that I see."

"I'm a blasphemer," Vosper repeated to the Saint, with a sort of derisive pride combined with the ponderous bonhomie of a vaudeville old-timer in a routine with a talking dog. He looked back up at the figure of the white-robed mystic towering above him, and said: "So if you have this direct pipeline to the Almighty, why don't you strike me dead?"

"Life and death are not in my hands," Astron said, in a calm and confident voice. "Death can only come from the hands of the Giver of all Life. In His own good time He will strike you down, and the arrow of God will silence your mockeries. This I have seen in the stars."

"Quaint, isn't he?" Vosper said, and opened the gate between the wall and the beach.

Beyond the wall a few steps led down to a kind of Grecian courtyard open on the seaward side, where the paving merged directly into the white sand of the beach. The courtyard was furnished with gaily-coloured lounging chairs and a well-stocked pushcart bar, to which Vosper immediately directed himself.

"You have visitors, Lucy," he said, without letting it interfere with the important work of reviving his highball.

Out on the sand, on a towel spread under an enormous beach umbrella, Mrs Herbert Wexall rolled over and said: "Oh, Mr Templar."

Simon went over and shook hands with her as she stood up.

46

It was hard to think of her as Janet Blaise's sister, for there were at least twenty years between them and hardly any physical resemblances. She was a big woman with an open, homely face and patchily sun-bleached hair and a sloppy figure, but she made a virtue of those disadvantages by the cheerfulness with which she ignored them. She was what is rather inadequately known as 'a person', which means that she had the personality to dispense with appearances and the money to back it up.

"Good to see you," she said, and turned to the man who had been sitting beside her, as he struggled to his feet. "Do you know Arthur Gresson?"

Mr Gresson was a full head shorter than the Saint's six foot two, but he weighed a good deal more. Unlike anyone else that Simon had encountered on the premises so far, his skin looked as if it was accustomed to exposure. His round body and his round balding brow, under a liberal sheen of oil, had the hot, rosy blush which the kiss of the sun evokes in virgin epidermis.

"Glad to meet you, Mr Templar." His hand was soft and earnestly adhesive.

"I expect you'd like a drink," Lucy Wexall said. "Let's keep Floyd working."

They joined Vosper at the bar wagon, and after he had started to work on the orders she turned back to the Saint and said: "After this formal service, just make yourself at home. I'm so glad you could come."

"I'm sure Mr Templar will be happy," Vosper said. "He's a man of the world like I am. We enjoy Lucy's food and liquor, and in return we give her the pleasure of hitting the society columns with our names. A perfectly businesslike exchange."

"That's progress for you," Lucy Wexall said breezily. "In the old days I'd have had a court jester. Now all I get is a professional stinker."

"That's no way to refer to Arthur," Vosper said, handing Simon a long, cold glass. "For your information, Templar, Mr Gresson – Mr Arthur *Granville* Gresson – is a promoter. He has a long history of selling phony oil stock behind him. He is just about to take Herb Wexall for another sucker; but since Herb married Lucy he can afford it. Unless you're sure you can

47

take Janet away from Reggie, I advise you not to listen to him."

Arthur Gresson's elbow nudged Simon's ribs.

"What a character!" he said, almost proudly.

"I only give out with facts," Vosper said. "My advice to you, Templar, is, never to be an elephant. Resist all inducements. Because when you reach back into that memory, you will only be laughed at, and the people who should thank you will call you a stinker."

Gresson giggled, deep from his round pink stomach.

"Would you like to get in a swim before lunch?" Lucy Wexall said. "Floyd, show him where he can change."

"A pleasure," Vosper said. "And probably a legitimate part of the bargain."

He thoughtfully refilled his glass before he steered Simon by way of the veranda into the beachward side of the house, and into a bedroom. He sat on the bed and watched unblinkingly while Simon stripped down and pulled on the trunks he had brought with him.

"It must be nice to have the Body Beautiful," he observed. "Of course, in your business it almost ranks with plant and machinery, doesn't it?"

The Saint's blue eyes twinkled.

"The main difference," he agreed good humouredly, "is that if I get a screw loose it may not be so noticeable."

As they were starting back through the living-room a small birdlike man in a dark and (for the setting outside the broad picture window) incongruous business suit bustled in by another door. He had the bright, baggy eyes behind rimless glasses, the slack but fleshless jowls, and the wide tight mouth which may not be common to all lawyers, bankers, and business executives, but which is certainly found in very few other vocations; and he was followed by a statuesque brunette whose severe tailoring failed to disguise an outstanding combination of curves, who carried a notebook and a sheaf of papers.

"Herb!" Vosper said. "I want you to meet Lucy's latest addition to the menagerie which already contains Astron and me – Mr Simon Templar, known as the Saint. Templar – your host, Mr Wexall."

"Pleased to meet you," said Herbert Wexall, shaking hands briskly.

"And this is Pauline Stone," Vosper went on, indicating the nubile brunette. "The tired business man's consolation. Whatever Lucy can't supply, she can."

"How do you do?" said the girl stoically.

Her dark eyes lingered momentarily on the Saint's torso, and he noticed that her mouth was very full and soft.

"Going for a swim?" Wexall said, as if he had heard nothing. "Good. Then I'll see you at lunch in a few minutes."

He trotted busily on his way, and Vosper ushered the Saint to the beach by another flight of steps that led directly down from the veranda. The house commanded a small half moon bay, and both ends of the crescent of sand were naturally guarded by abrupt rises of jagged coral rock.

"Herbert is the living example of how really stupid a successful business man can be," Vosper said tirelessly. "He was just an office boy of some kind in the Blaise outfit when he got smart enough to woo and win the boss's daughter. And from that flying start he was clever enough to really pay his way by making Blaise Industries twice as big as even the old man himself had been able to do. And yet he's dumb enough to think that Lucy won't catch on to the extra-curricular functions of that busty secretary sooner or later – or that when she does he won't be out on a cold doorstep in the rain. . . . No, I'm not going in. I'll hold your drink for you."

Simon ran down into the surf and churned seawards for a couple of hundred yards, then turned over and paddled lazily back, co-ordinating his impressions with idle amusement. The balmy water was still refreshing after the heat of the morning, and when he came out the breeze had become brisk enough to give him the luxury of a fleeting shiver as the wetness started to evaporate from his tanned skin.

He crossed the sand to the Greek patio, where Floyd Vosper was on duty again at the bar in a strategic position to keep his own needs supplied with a minimum of effort. Discreet servants were setting up a buffet table. Janet Blaise and Reg Herrick had transferred their gin rummy game and were playing

49

at a table right under the column where Astron had resumed his seat and his cataleptic meditations – a weird juxtaposition of which the three members all seemed equally unconscious.

Simon took Lucy Wexall a Martini and said with another glance at the tableau: "Where did you find him?"

"The people who brought him to California sent him to me when he had to leave the States. They gave me such a good time when I was out there, I couldn't refuse to do something for them. He's writing a book, you know, and, of course, can't go back to that dreadful place he came from, wherever it is, before he has a chance to finish it in reasonable comfort."

Simon avoided discussing this assumption, but he said: "What's it like, having a resident prophet in the house?"

"He's very interesting. And quite as drastic as Floyd, in his own way, in summing up people. You ought to talk to him."

Arthur Gresson came over with a *hors d'œuvre* plate of smoked salmon and stuffed eggs from the buffet. He said: "Anyone you meet at Lucy's is interesting, Mr Templar. But if you don't mind my saying so, you have it all over the rest of 'em. Who'd ever think we'd find the Saint looking for crime in the Bahamas?"

"I hope no one will think I'm looking for crime," Simon said deprecatingly, "any more than I take it for granted that you're looking for oil."

"That's where you'd be wrong," Gresson said. "As a matter of fact, I am."

The Saint raised an eyebrow.

"Well, I can always learn something. I'd never heard of oil in the Bahamas."

"I'm not a bit surprised. But you will, Mr Templar, you will." Gresson sat down, pillowing his round stomach on his thighs. "Just think for a moment about some of the places you have heard of, where there is certainly oil. Let me mention them in a certain order. Mexico, Texas, Louisiana, and the recent strike in the Florida Everglades. We might even include Venezuela in the south. Does that suggest anything to you?"

"Hm – mm," said the Saint thoughtfully.

"A pattern," Gresson said. "A vast central pool of oil somewhere under the Gulf of Mexico, with oil wells dipping into it from the edges of the bowl, where the geological strata have also been forced up. Now think of the islands of the Caribbean as the eastern edge of the same bowl. Why not?"

"It's a hell of an interesting theory," said the Saint.

"Mr Wexal thinks so, too, and I hope he's going into partnership with me."

"Herbert can afford it," intruded the metallic sneering voice of Floyd Vosper. "But before you decide to buy in, Templar, you'd better check with New York about the time when Mr Gresson thought he could dig gold in the Catskills."

"Shut up, Floyd," said Mrs Wexall, "and get me another Martini."

Arthur Granville Gresson chuckled in his paunch like a happy Buddha.

"What a guy!" he said. "What a ribber! And he gets everyone mad. He kills me!"

Herbert Wexall came down from the veranda and beamed around. As a sort of taciturn announcement that he had put aside his work for the day, he had changed into a sports shirt on which various exotic fish were depicted wandering through vines of seaweed, but he retained his business trousers and business shoes and business face.

"Well," he said, inspecting the buffet and addressing the world at large. "Let's come and get it whenever we're hungry."

As if a spell had been snapped, Astron removed himself from the contemplation of the infinite, descended from his pillar, and began to help himself to cottage cheese and caviar on a foundation of lettuce leaves.

Simon drifted in the same direction, and found Pauline Stone beside him, saying: "What do you feel like, Mr Templar?"

Her indication of having come off duty was a good deal more radical than her employer's. In fact, the bathing suit which she had changed into seemed to be based on the French minima of the period than on any British tradition. There was no doubt that she filled it opulently; and her question amplified its suggestiveness with undertones which the Saint felt it wiser not to challenge at that moment.

"There's so much to drool over," he said, referring studiously to the buffet table. "But that green turtle aspic looks pretty good to me."

She stayed with him when he carried his plate to a table as thoughtfully diametric as possible from the berth chosen by Floyd Vosper, even though Astron had already settled there in temporary solitude. They were promptly joined by Reg Herrick and Janet Blaise, and slipped at once into an easy exchange of banalities.

But even then it was impossible to escape Vosper's tongue. It was not many minutes before his saw-edged voice whined across the patio above the general level of harmless chatter:

"When are you going to tell the Saint's fortune, Astron? That ought to be worth hearing."

There was a slightly embarrassed lull, and then everyone went on talking again; but Astron looked at the Saint with a gentle smile and said quietly: "You are a seeker after truth; Mr Templar, as I am. But when instead of truth you find falsehood you will destroy it with a sword. I only say 'This is falsehood, and God will destroy it. Do not come too close, lest you be destroyed with it.' "

"Okay," Herrick growled, just as quietly. "But if you're talking about Vosper, it's about time someone destroyed it."

"Sometimes," Astron said, "God places His arrow in the hand of a man."

For a few moments that seemed unconscionably long nobody said anything; and then, before the silence spread beyond their small group, the Saint said casually: "Talking of arrows – I hear that the sport this season is to go hunting sharks with a bow and arrow."

Herrick nodded with a healthy grin.

"It's a lot of fun. Would you like to try it?"

"Reggie's terrific," Janet Blaise said. "He shoots like a regular Howard Hill, but, of course, he uses a bow that nobody else can pull."

"I'd like to try," said the Saint, and the conversation slid harmlessly along the tangent he had provided.

After lunch everyone went back to the beach, with the

exception of Astron, who retired to put his morning's meditations on paper. Chatter surrendered to an afternoon torpor which even subdued Vosper.

An indefinite while later, Herrick aroused with a yell and plunged roaring into the sea, followed by Janet Blaise. They were followed by others, including the Saint. An interlude of aquatic brawling developed somehow into a pickup game of touch football on the beach, which was delightfully confused by recurrent arguments about who was supposed to be on which of the unequal sides. This boisterous nonsense churned up enough sand for the still freshening breeze to spray over Floyd Vosper, who by that time had drunk enough to be trying to sleep under the big beach umbrella, and finally to get the misanthropic oracle back on his feet.

"Perhaps," he said witheringly, "I had better get out of the way of you perennial juveniles before you convert me into a dune."

He stalked off along the beach and lay down again about a hundred yards away. Simon noticed him still there, flat on his face and presumably unconscious, when the game eventually broke up through a confused water-polo phase to leave everyone gasping and laughing and dripping on the patio with no immediate resurge of inspiration. It was the last time he saw the unpopular Mr Vosper alive.

"Well," Arthur Gresson observed, mopping his short round body with a towel, "at least one of us seems to have enough sense to know when to lie down."

"And to choose the only partner who'd do it with him," Pauline added vaguely.

Herbert Wexall glanced along the beach in the direction that they both referred to, then glanced for further inspiration at the waterproof watch he was still wearing.

"It's almost cocktail time," he said. "How about it, anyone?"

His wife shivered and said: "I'm starting to freeze my tail off. It's going to blow like a son-of-a-gun any minute. Let's all go in and get some clothes on first – then we'll be set for the evening. You'll stay for supper, of course, Mr Templar?"

"I hadn't planned to make a day of it," Simon protested diffidently, and was promptly overwhelmed from all quarters.

He found his way back to the room where he had left his clothes without the benefit of Floyd Vosper's chatty courier service, and made leisured and satisfactory use of the fresh-water shower and monogrammed towels. Even so, when he sauntered back into the living-room, he almost had the feeling of being lost in a strange and empty house, for all the varied individuals who had peopled the stage so vividly and vigorously a short time before had vanished into other and unknown seclusions and had not yet returned.

He lighted a cigarette and strolled idly towards the picture window that overlooked the veranda and the sea. Everything around his solitude was so still, excepting the subsonic suggestion of distant movements within the house, that he was tempted to walk on tiptoe; and yet outside the broad pane of plate glass the fronds of coconut palms were fluttering in a thin febrile frenzy, and there were lacings of white cream on the incredible jade of the short waves simmering on the beach.

He noticed first, in what should have been a lazily sensual survey of the panorama, that the big beach umbrella was no longer where he had first seen it, down to his right outside the pseudo-Grecian patio. He saw, as his eye wandered on, that it had been moved a hundred yards or so to his left – in fact to the very place where Floyd Vosper was still lying. It occurred to him first that Vosper must have moved it himself, except that no shade was needed in the brief and darkening twilight. After that he noticed that Vosper seemed to have turned over on his back; and then at last as the Saint focused his eyes he saw with a weird thrill that the shaft of the umbrella stood straight up out of the left side of Vosper's scrawny brown chest, not in the sand beside him at all, but like a gigantic pin that had impaled a strange and inelegant insect – or, in a fantastic phrase that was not Simon's at all – like the arrow of God.

MAJOR RUPERT FANSHIRE, the senior Superintendent of Police, which made him third in the local hierarchy after the Commissioner and the Deputy Commissioner, paid tribute to the importance of the case by taking personal charge of it. He was a slight pinkish blond man with rather large and very bright blue eyes, and such a discreetly modulated voice that it commanded rapt attention through the basic effort of trying to hear what it was saying. He sat at an ordinary writing desk in the living-room, with a Bahamian sergeant standing stiffly beside him, and contrived to turn the whole room into an office in which seven previously happy-go-lucky adults wriggled like guilty school children whose teacher has been found libellously caricatured on their blackboard.

He said, with wholly impersonal conciseness: "Of course, you all know by now that Mr Vosper was found on the beach with the steel spike of an umbrella through his chest. My job is to find out how it happened. So to start with, if anyone did it to him, the topography suggests that that person came from, or through, this house. I've heard all your statements, and all they seem to amount to is that each of you was going about his own business at the time when this might have happened."

"All I know," Herbert Wexall said, "is that I was in my study, reading and signing the letters that I dictated this morning."

"And I was getting dressed," said his wife.

"So was I," said Janet Blaise.

"I guess I was in the shower," said Reginald Herrick.

"I was having a bubble bath," said Pauline Stone.

"I was still working," said Astron. "This morning I started a new chapter of my book – in my mind, you understand. I do not write by putting everything on paper. For me it is necessary to meditate, to feel, to open floodgates in my mind, so that I can receive the wisdom that comes from beyond the—"

"Quite," Major Fanshire assented politely. "The point is

that none of you have alibis, if you need them. You were all going about your own business, in your own rooms. Mr Templar was changing in the late Mr Vosper's room—"

"I wasn't here," Arthur Gresson said recklessly. "I drove back to my own place – I'm staying at the Fort Montagu Beach Hotel. I wanted a clean shirt. I drove back there, and when I came back here all this had happened."

"There's not much difference," Major Fanshire said. "Dr Rassin tells me we couldn't establish the time of death within an hour or two, anyway. . . . So the next thing we come to is the question of motive. Did anyone here," Fanshire said almost innocently, "have any really serious trouble with Mr Vosper?"

There was an uncomfortable silence, which the Saint finally broke by saying: "I'm on the outside here, so I'll take the rap. I'll answer for everyone."

The Superintendent cocked his bright eyes.

"Very well, sir. What would you say?"

"My answer," said the Saint, "is – everybody."

There was another silence, but a very different one, in which it seemed, surprisingly, as if all of them relaxed as unanimously as they had stiffened before. And yet, in its own way, this relaxation was as self-conscious and uncomfortable as the preceding tension had been. Only the Saint, who had every attitude of the completely careless onlooker, and Major Fanshire, whose deferential patience was impregnably correct, seemed immune to the interplay of hidden strains.

"Would you care to go any further?" Fanshire asked.

"Certainly," said the Saint. "I'll go anywhere. I can say what I like, and I don't have to care whether anyone is on speaking terms with me tomorrow. I'll go on record with my opinion that the late Mr Vosper was one of the most unpleasant characters I've ever met. I'll make the statement, if it isn't already general knowledge, that he made a speciality of needling everyone he spoke to or about. He goaded everyone with nasty little things that he knew, or thought he knew, about them. I wouldn't blame anyone here for wanting, at least theoretically, to kill him."

"I'm not exactly concerned with your interpretation of

blame," Fanshire said detachedly. "But if you have any facts, I'd like to hear them."

"I have no facts," said the Saint coolly. "I only know that in the few hours I've been here Vosper made statements to me, a stranger, about everyone here, any one of which could be called fighting words."

"You will have to be more specific," Fanshire said.

"Okay," said the Saint. "I apologize in advance to anyone it hurts. Remember, I'm only repeating the kind of thing that made Vosper a good murder candidate. . . . I am now specific. In my hearing, he called Reg Herrick a dumb athlete who was trying to marry Janet Blaise for her money. He suggested that Janet was a stupid juvenile for taking him seriously. He called Astron a commercial charlatan. He implied that Lucy Wexall was a dope and a snob. He inferred that Herb Wexall had more use for his secretary's sex than for her stenography, and he thought out loud that Pauline was amenable. He called Mr Gresson a crook to his face."

"And during all this," Fanshire said, with an inoffensiveness that had to be heard to be believed, "he said nothing about you?"

"He did indeed," said the Saint. "He analysed me, more or less, as a flamboyant phony."

"And you didn't object to that?"

"I hardly could," Simon replied blandly, "after I'd hinted to him that I thought he was even phonier."

It was a line on which a stage audience could have tittered, but the tensions of the moment let it sink with a slow thud.

Fanshire drew down his upper lip with one forefinger and nibbled it inscrutably.

"I expect this bores you as much as it does me, but this is the job I'm paid for. I've got to say that all of you had the opportunity, and from what Mr Templar says you could all have had some sort of motive. Well, now I've got to look into what you might call the problem of physical possibility."

Simon Templar lighted a cigarette. It was the only movement that anyone made, and after that he was the most intent listener of them all as Fanshire went on:

"Dr Rassin says, and I must say I agree with him, that to drive that umbrella shaft clean through a man's chest must have taken quite exceptional strength. It seems to be something that no woman, and probably no ordinary man, could have done."

His pale bright eyes came to rest on Herrick as he finished speaking, and the Saint found his own eyes following others in the same direction.

The picture formed in his mind, the young giant towering over a prostrate Vosper, the umbrella raised in his mighty arms like a fantastic spear and the setting sun flaming on his red head, like an avenging angel, and the thrust downwards with all the power of those herculean shoulders . . . and then, as Herrick's face began to flush under the awareness of so many stares, Janet Blaise suddenly cried out: "No! No – it couldn't have been Reggie!"

Fanshire's gaze transferred itself to her curiously, and she said in a stammering rush: "You see, it's silly, but we didn't quite tell the truth, I mean about being in our own rooms. As a matter of fact Reggie was in my room most of the time. We were – talking."

The Superintendent cleared his throat and continued to gaze at her stolidly for a while. He didn't make any comment. But presently he looked at the Saint in the same dispassionately thoughtful way that he had first looked at Herrick.

Simon said calmly: "Yes, I was just wondering myself whether I could have done it. And I had a rather interesting thought."

"Yes, Mr Templar?"

"Certainly it must take quite a lot of strength to drive a spike through a man's chest with one blow. But now remember that this wasn't just a spike, or a spear. It had an enormous great umbrella on top of it. Now think what would happen if you were stabbing down with a thing like that?"

"Well, what would happen?"

"The umbrella would be like a parachute. It would be like a sort of sky anchor holding the shaft back. The air resistance would be so great that I'm wondering how anyone, even a very strong man, could get much momentum into the thrust. And the more force he put into it, the more likely he'd be to lift himself off the ground, rather than drive the spike down."

Fanshire digested this, blinking, and took his full time to do it.

"That certainly is a thought," he admitted. "But damn it," he exploded, "we know it was done. So it must have been possible."

"There's something entirely backwards about that logic," said the Saint. "Suppose we say, if it was impossible, maybe it wasn't done."

"Now you're being a little ridiculous," Fanshire snapped. "We saw——"

"We saw a man with the sharp iron-tipped shaft of a beach umbrella through his chest. We jumped to the natural conclusion that somebody stuck it into him like a sword. And that may be just what a clever murderer meant us to think."

Then it was Arthur Gresson who shattered the fragile silence by leaping out of his chair like a bouncing ball.

"I've got it!" he yelped. "Believe me, everybody, I've got it! This'll kill you!"

"I hope not," Major Fanshire said dryly. "But what is it?"

"Listen," Gresson said. "I knew something rang a bell somewhere, but I couldn't place it. Now it all comes back to me. This is something I only heard at the hotel the other day, but some of you must have heard it before. It happened a year ago, when Gregory Peck was visiting here. He stayed at the same hotel where I am, and one afternoon he was on the beach, and the wind came up, just like it did today, and it picked up one of those beach umbrellas and carried it right to where he was lying, and the point just grazed his ribs and gave him a nasty gash, but what the people who saw it happen were saying was that if it'd been just a few inches the other way, it could have gone smack into his heart, and you'd've had a film star killed in the most sensational way that ever was. Didn't you ever hear about that, Major?"

"Now you mention it," Fanshire said slowly, "I think I did hear something about it."

"Well," Gresson said, "*what if it happened again this afternoon, to someone who wasn't as lucky as Peck?*"

There was another of those electric silences of assimilation, out of which Lucy Wexall said: "Yes, I heard about that." And Janet said: "Remember, I told you about it! I was visiting some friends at the hotel that day, and I didn't see it happen, but I was there for the commotion."

Gresson spread out his arms, his round face gleaming with excitement and perspiration.

"That's got to be it!" he said. "You remember how Vosper was lying under the umbrella outside the patio when we started playing touch football, and he got sore because we were kicking sand over him, and he went off to the other end of the beach? But he didn't take the umbrella with him. The wind did that, after we all went off to change. And this time it didn't miss!"

Suddenly Astron stood up beside him; but where Gresson had risen like a jumping bean, this was like the growth and unfolding of a tree.

"I have heard many words," Astron said in his firm, gentle voice, "but now at last I think I am hearing truth. No man struck the blasphemer down. The arrow of God smote him, in his wickedness and his pride, as it was written long ago in the stars."

"You can say that again," Gresson proclaimed triumphantly. "He sure had it coming."

Again the Saint drew at his cigarette and created his own vision behind half closed eyes. He saw the huge umbrella plucked from the sand by the invisible fingers of the wind, picked up and hurled spinning along the deserted twilight beach, its great mushroom spread of gaudy canvas no longer a drag now, but a sail for the wind to get behind, the whole thing transformed into a huge unearthly dart flung with literally superhuman power, the arrow of God indeed. A fantastic, an almost unimaginable solution; and yet it did not have to be imagined because there were witnesses that it had actually almost happened once before. . . .

Fanshire was saying: "By Jove, that's the best suggestion I've heard yet – without any religious implication, of course. It sounds as if it could be the right answer!"

Simon's eyes opened on him fully for an instant, almost pityingly, and then closed completely as the true and right and complete answer rolled through the Saint's mind like a long peaceful wave.

"I have one question to ask," said the Saint.

"What's that?" Fanshire said, too politely to be irritable, yet with a trace of impatience, as if he hated the inconvenience of even defending such a divinely tailored theory.

"Does anyone here have a gun?" asked the Saint.

There was an almost audible creaking of knitted brows, and Fanshire said: "Really, Mr Templar, I don't quite follow you."

"I only asked," said the Saint imperturbably, "if anyone here had a gun. I'd sort of like to know the answer before I explain why."

"I have a revolver," Wexall said with some perplexity. "What about it?"

"Could we see it, please?" said the Saint.

"I'll get it," said Pauline Stone.

She got up and left the room.

"You know I have a gun, Fanshire," Wexall said. "You gave me my permit. But I don't see—"

"Neither do I," Fanshire said.

The Saint said nothing. He devoted himself to his cigarette, with impregnable detachment, until the voluptuous secretary came back. Then he put out the cigarette and extended his hand.

Pauline looked at Wexall, hesitantly, and at Fanshire. The Superintendent nodded a sort of grudging acquiescence. Simon took the gun and broke it expertly.

"A Colt .38 Detective Special," he said. "Unloaded." He sniffed the barrel. "But fired quite recently," he said, and handed the gun to Fanshire.

"I used it myself this morning," Lucy Wexall said cheerfully. "Janet and Reg and I were shooting at the Portuguese men-of-war. There were quite a lot of them around before the breeze came up."

"I wondered what the noise was," Wexall said vaguely.

"I was coming up the drive when I heard it first," Gresson said, "and I thought the next war had started."

"This is all very interesting," Fanshire said, removing the revolver barrel from the proximity of his nostrils with a trace of exasperation, "but I don't see what it has to do with the case. Nobody has been shot—"

"Major Fanshire," said the Saint quietly, "may I have a word with you outside? And will you keep that gun in your pocket so that at least we can hope there will be no more shooting?"

The Superintendent stared at him for several seconds, and at last unwillingly got up.

"Very well, Mr Templar." He stuffed the revolver into the side pocket of his rumpled white jacket, and glanced back at his impassive chocolate sentinel. "Sergeant, see that nobody leaves here, will you?"

He followed Simon out on to the veranda and said almost peremptorily: "Come on now, what's this all about?"

It was so much like a flash of a faraway Scotland Yard Inspector that the Saint had to control a smile. But he took Fanshire's arm and led him persuasively down the front steps to the beach. Off to their left a tiny red glow-worm blinked low down under the silver stars.

"You still have somebody watching the place where the body was found," Simon said.

"Of course," Fanshire grumbled. "As a matter of routine. But the sand's much too soft to show any footprints, and—"

"Will you walk over there with me?"

Fanshire sighed briefly, and trudged beside him. His politeness was dogged but unfailing. He was a type that had been schooled from adolescence never to give up, even to the ultimate in ennui. In the interests of total fairness, he would be game to the last yawn.

He did go so far as to say: "I don't know what you're getting at, but why *couldn't* it have been an accident?"

"I never heard a better theory in my life," said the Saint equably, "with one insuperable flaw."

"What's that?"

"Only," said the Saint, very gently, "that the wind wasn't blowing the right way."

Major Fanshire kept his face straight ahead to the wind and said nothing more after that until they reached the glow-worm that they were making for and it became a cigarette end that a constable dropped as he came to attention.

The place where Floyd Vosper had been lying was marked off in a square of tape, but there was nothing out of the ordinary about it except some small stains that showed almost black under the flashlight which the constable produced.

"May I mess up the scene a bit?" Simon asked.

"I don't see why not," Fanshire said doubtfully. "It doesn't show anything, really."

Simon went down on his knees and began to dig with his hands, around and under the place where the stains were. Minutes later he stood up, with sand tricking through his fingers, and showed Fanshire the mushroomed scrap of metal that he had found.

"A .38 bullet," Fanshire said, and whistled.

"And I think you'll be able to prove it was fired from the gun you have in your pocket," said the Saint. "Also you'd better have a sack of sand picked up from where I was digging. I think a laboratory examination will find that it also contains fragments of bone and human flesh."

"You'll have to explain this to me," Fanshire said quite humbly.

Simon dusted his hands and lighted a cigarette.

"Vosper was lying on his face when I last saw him," he said, "and I think he was as much passed out as sleeping. With the wind and the surf and the soft sand, it was easy for the murderer to creep up on him and shoot him in the back where he lay. But the murderer didn't want you looking for guns and comparing bullets. The umbrella was the inspiration. I don't have to remind you that the exit hole of a bullet is much larger than the entrance. By turning Vosper's body over, the murderer found a hole in his chest that it can't have been too difficult to force the umbrella shaft through – obliterating the original wound and confusing everybody in one simple operation."

"Let's get back to the house," said the Superintendent abruptly.

After a while, as they walked, Fanshire said: "It's going to feel awfully funny having to arrest Herbert Wexall."

"Good God!" said the Saint in honest astonishment. "You weren't thinking of doing that?"

Fanshire stopped and blinked at him under the still distant light of the uncurtained windows.

"Why not?"

"Did Herbert seem at all guilty when he admitted he had a gun? Did he seem at all uncomfortable – I don't mean just puzzled, like you were – about having it produced? Was he ready with the explanation of why it still smelled of being fired?"

"But if anyone else used Wexall's gun," Fanshire pondered laboriously, "why should they go to such lengths to make it look as if no gun was used at all, when Wexall would obviously have been suspected?"

"Because it was somebody who didn't want Wexall to take the rap," said the Saint. "Because Wexall is the goose who could still lay golden eggs – but he wouldn't do much laying on the end of a rope, or whatever you do to murderers here."

The Superintendent pulled out a handkerchief and wiped his face.

"My God," he said, "you mean you think Lucy—"

"I think we have to go all the way back to the prime question of motive," said the Saint. "Floyd Vosper was a nasty man who made dirty cracks about everyone here. But his cracks were dirtiest because he always had a wickedly good idea what he was talking about. Nevertheless, very few people become murderers because of a dirty crack. Very few people except me kill other people on points of principle. Vosper called us all variously dupes, phonies, cheaters and fools. But since he had roughly the same description for all of us, we could all laugh it off. There was one person about whom he made the unforgivable accusation. . . . Now shall we rejoin the mob?"

"You'd better do this your own way," Fanshire muttered.

Simon Templar took him up the steps to the veranda and back through the french doors into the living-room, where all eyes turned to them in deathly silence.

"A paraffin test will prove who fired that revolver in the last twenty-four hours, aside from those who have already admitted it," Simon said, as if there had been no interruption. "And you'll remember, I'm sure, who supplied that very handy theory about the arrow of God."

"Astron!" Fanshire gasped.

"Oh, no," said the Saint, a little tiredly. "He only said that God sometimes places His arrow in the hands of a man. And I feel quite sure that a wire to New York will establish that there is actually a criminal file under the name of Granville, with fingerprints and photos that should match Mr Gresson's – as Vosper's fatally elephantine memory remembered. . . . That was the one crack he shouldn't have made, because it was the only one that was more than gossip or shrewd insult, the only one that could be easily proved, and the only one that had a chance of upsetting an operation which was all set – if you'll excuse the phrase – to make a big killing."

Major Fanshire fingered his upper lip.

"I don't know," he began; and then, as Arthur Granville Gresson began to rise like a floating balloon from his chair, and the ebony-faced sergeant moved to intercept him like a well-disciplined automaton, he knew.

— JAMAICA —

THE BLACK COMMISSAR

THE WHITE crescent of Montego Bay was under their wings, and most of the passengers on the Pan American Clipper who were disembarking at Kingston could be identified by a certain purposeful stirring as they straightened and reassembled themselves and their impedimenta in preparation for the landing a few minutes ahead. Simon Templar, who saw no reason for not travelling from one vacation spot to another in vacation clothes, was ready for Jamaica without further preparation, wearing nothing more troublesome than sandals, slacks, and a sports shirt tastefully decorated with a pattern of rainbow-hued tropical fish circulating through a forest of graceful corals and vivid submarine flora; but he calculated that he had time for one more cigarette before the 'no-smoking' sign went on, and lighted it without haste.

The woman who had been sitting next to him, a cold-eyed and stoutly corseted dowager of the type which travel agencies so skilfully keep out of the pictures in their romantically illustrated brochures, had temporarily left her seat, presumably for basic adjustments in the privacy of the ladies' room, and Simon thought it was only she returning when he felt someone loom over him and settle in the adjoining chair. He continued to gaze idly at the scenery below his window until a voice brought his head around – rather abruptly, because not only had that forbidding female maintained a majestic silence throughout the trip, but the voice was much deeper than even she could plausibly have possessed, and moreover it addressed him by name.

"Excuse me, Mr Saint, sah."

Simon looked into a grinning ebony face that was puzzlingly familiar, but which he somehow couldn't associate at all with the spotless white shirt, port-wine shantung jacket, hand-painted tie, and smartly creased dove-grey trousers which the young negro wore.

"Bet you didn't recognize me, sah."

Simon felt a little embarrassed, more so than if a white man had posed him the same challenge, but he smiled amiably.

"Yes, I know I've seen you before. But where?"

"Johnny, sah. I was a sparrin' partner with Steve Nelson, up in New York, the time you and he had that go with the Masked Angel. Remember now, Mr Saint?"

"Of course." Now it all came back. "But go easy with that name, will you? I'm trying to live a quiet and peaceful life for a while."

"I'm sorry, sah."

"I don't think anyone else is. . . . Well, I've certainly got an excuse for not recognizing you. I don't think I ever saw you before with anything but trunks on. What are you doing now, and where are you going?"

"Home, sah."

The Saint raised his eyebrows with pleasant interest, but he could not escape a faint flicker of guilt that touched him at a deeper level. Of course he remembered Johnny: a nice, well-mannered, good natured, hardworking coloured boy around the gym, a willing but not gifted fighter . . . and that was all. As a being of a different race and colour, his background, his past, his personal private present and his unpredictable future, had seemed as remote and insignificant, except as they might affect any immediate contact with him, as the private life of a mounted policeman's horse. It was strange how incurious one could be about any fellow human, especially one whose complexion made him an everlasting stranger.

"Home?" said the Saint. "Where's that?"

"Jamaica, sah. I was born here." The man added, with an odd touch of pride: "I'm a Maroon."

Perhaps hardly one listener in ten thousand would have had any answer but the equivalent of 'What?' or 'So what?' to such a statement, but Simon Templar was that one. It was one of those coincidences that were almost commonplace in his life that he not only knew what a Maroon was, but even had some elements of an immediate interest in that little-known political survival of the old wild history of the West Indies.

Johnny, however, had already interpreted the Saint's minuscule stiffening of surprise as a normal reaction of perplexity, and was hastening to explain: "The original Maroons were slaves who ran away, back at the beginnin' of the eighteenth century, an' took to the hills. When there was enough of 'em, they kept fightin' the British troops who tried to round 'em up, till it was just like a war. They done so well that finally the British Empire had to give up an' make a peace treaty with 'em."

"I've heard about them," said the Saint. "They got their freedom, and a piece of the island set aside for them and their descendants for ever, sort of like an Indian reservation in the States. Only I was told that they make their own laws and appoint their own rulers and nobody can interfere with them in any way, just as if they were an independent little country of their own."

"That's right," Johnny said. "And that's our country, right underneath you now."

Simon looked down through the window. Below them was a welter of steeply rounded hills, reminiscent in shape of a mass of old-fashioned beehives jampacked together. Over almost every foot of surface the jungle grew like a coat of curly green wool above which only the top of the tallest trees raised little knots like the mounds in a pebble-weave fabric. Only here and there was the denseness broken by a smoother slope that seemed to be open grass, a tiny brown patch of cultivation, the shiny specks of a banana patch, or the silver thread of a stream exposed on an outcropping of bare boulders; but most of it looked as wild and impenetrable as any terrain that the Saint had ever seen.

"They call it the Cockpit," Johnny said. "I dunno why, 'cept that it's sure seen a lot of fightin'. Doesn't look like it's changed much, though I was only twelve when my dad took me away to the States."

"What makes you want to go back?" Simon asked.

"Well, sah, he died soon after that, so I didn't get to go to

68

school much more. I was too busy hustlin' for a livin'. Bein' a sparrin' partner was just another job. When I found I didn't have what it takes to be a top fighter, I gave that up. I done all kinds of things, from shoeshine boy to cook an' butler. But by the time I met you I'd decided I wanted to be something better, an' I started savin' my money an' goin' to night school. Presently I learned enough an' saved up enough to pass the entrance exam to Tuskegee an' afford to go there. Got me a degree a year ago. I know I'll never talk like a college man, that's a bad habit I've had too long, but I sure learned all I could."

"You've got enough to be proud of," said the Saint. "But that still doesn't tell me why you aren't going on from there to something better in the States."

"Well, sah, you know as well as I do how it is up there. There's a limit to what a coloured man can do." Johnny spoke with devastating candour, without inferiority or rancour. "Some of the fellows at college always think they're goin' to change the world. I never felt big enough for that; but I done plenty of thinkin'. After I got out an' tried it, I knew I was always goin' to have to just be the best I could among coloured people. So then I began thinkin', well, if that's how it is, why don't I go back an' do that with my own coloured people, the Maroons, where I came from? Maybe I'm needed more down here, where some negroes go to English universities, but others are more illiterate even than the poorest share-cropper in Mississippi. . . . I dunno, I thought, maybe I can help more of 'em to be ready when that change in the world comes."

The sincerity in his brown eyes was so cloudless and complete that Simon found himself hopelessly assaying a medley of assorted answers, afraid to utter any of them spontaneously lest he sound smug and patronizing.

In that paralysis of fumbling sensitivity, the Deadly Dowager herself came to his rescue. Both Simon and Johnny simultaneously became aware of her, freshly girdled and painted, lowering over her usurped seat and transfixing them alternately with the daggers of her arctic eyes.

Even before the Saint himself could adjust to that unexpected additional problem, Johnny was scrambling out of the chair with the ingrained quick defensive humility that not even a degree from Tuskegee had eradicated, that was somehow a subtle humiliation to both races.

"Excuse me, ma'am. And thank you for listenin', sah."

There was little that the Saint could do, the world not yet having changed. The illuminated sign on the forward bulkhead was on, and the stewardess was already intoning: "Will you fasten your seat belts, please? And no smoking, please." But little as it was, Simon did it.

He put out his hand, directly across the entering matriarch's mid-section.

"It was nice seeing you again, Johnny. Maybe I'll run into you again – in the Cockpit."

Then the dame surged like a tidal wave into her seat.

"Well!" she said, condensing innumerable volumes into a single syllable.

The Saint's only consolation was that for the remaining few minutes of the flight she stayed as far away from him as if he had been labelled the carrier of a contagious disease, which gave him a comfortable excess over the normally limited amount of elbow room.

2

D AVID FARNHAM was at the airport, a sturdy and unmistakably British figure in open-necked shirt and khaki walking shorts, pipe in mouth, bright eyes and bald head shining. Under his benevolent ægis the formalities of immigration and customs passed Simon through as if on a fast-rolling conveyor belt, and in a matter of mere minutes they were in Farnham's little English car, circling around the harbour and edging into the crowded clattering streets of the town.

"I hope my wire wasn't too much of a shock to you," said the Saint. "When you talked to me at that cocktail party in Nassau, you probaby never thought I'd take you up on your invitation."

"On the contrary, I'm delighted that you finally did. I always believed you would, and it's nice of you to prove I was right."

"I didn't expect you to meet me, though. Won't the Government mind your taking this time off?"

"Government has nothing to say about it," Farnham told him sedately. "I've managed to retire at last. They wanted me to carry on, but having reached the age of sixty they couldn't prevent me getting out. I've been looking forward to this for a long time."

Simon regarded him speculatively. He knew, although David by no means told everyone, that his host had been a school teacher before he had been practically drafted into the service of the Colonial Secretariat, on an indefinite leave of absence from his blackboard which had been extended for so long that his original calling was often forgotten. Placed in charge of almost every activity which could be classified under the broad heading of General Progress, he had brought so much honest enthusiasm and kindly wisdom to his job that the temporary appointment had driften into a *de facto* permanency.

"I still don't see you wearing a cap and gown," Simon remarked.

"Not that, either. I'm too old to start that all over again. I think I did my job just the same, even without a classroom. No, I'm retired. Some years ago we were able to pick up quite a bargain in a small farm in The Halt Way Tree area. We rise at six and retire well before nine, and our one excitement is a weekly trip to town for shopping, golf, supper, and cinema. It's a simple life, and we enjoy it very much. . . . However, I can still take you to visit the Maroons, as I promised."

"I'm still very interested," Simon said.

The western outskirts of Kingston merged into picturesque Spanish Town, and then they were through that and out on the rambling highway.

"In fact," said the Saint, lighting a cigarette, "I seem to keep on being reminded of the Maroons, as if Fate was determined to keep prodding me into something. Even on the plane coming in here, a few minutes before we landed, a coloured fellow spoke to me, whom I met years ago in New York, when he was earning his way towards college by working as sparring partner with a pugilist friend of mine; and it turns out he's on his way home, which is here – and damned if he didn't tell me he was a Maroon."

"What was his name?"

"Johnny. . . . You know, I'm ashamed to say it, but that's still all I know. Just Johnny."

"It could be his last name," Farnham said. "One of the leaders of the original Maroons was named Johnny."

Simon shrugged.

"But long before that, soon after I met you, and before I left Nassau, I ran into another bloke from Jamaica. Name of Jerry Dugdale."

"I remember him. He was in the police here."

"That's the guy. He repeated just what you'd told me, almost in the very same words, about how the Maroons had an ancient Treaty which gave them the right to make their own laws and set up their own government. Furthermore, he told me that once upon a time he was wanting to chat with a couple of natives about a slight case of murder, and he got word that they'd taken off for the Maroon country, so he went in to look for them; and the Maroon boss man complained to the Governor, and the Governor had Jerry on the carpet and chewed him out for violating their Treaty rights and almost making an international incident."

"It's quite possible," Farnham said. "The Maroons are very touchy about their privileges."

"Right then," said the Saint, "I guess I knew that this was something I had to see. A little independent state left over for a couple of centuries, right inside the island of Jamaica – that's something I could top any tourist story with."

"It certainly is unique, at least in the West Indies. But," Farnham said, without taking his eyes off the road, "I hardly thought you'd be so interested in topping tourist stories. You wouldn't perhaps have been specially intrigued by the fact that Dugdale wasn't allowed to chase his criminals in there, would you?"

"It does give it a sort of piquant slant," Simon admitted cheerfully. He looked at his companion again and said: "But from the point of view of your Government, a situation like that could have problems, couldn't it?"

"It could," Farnham said steadily. "And before you're much older I'll tell you about one."

It had taken rather a long time, so long that the Saint felt no electrifying change, only a deepening and enriched fulfilment of his faith in coincidences and the sure guiding hand of destiny.

But David Farnham seemed to feel as unhurried as destiny itself, and Simon did not press him. Now that he knew for certain that he had something to look forward to, the Saint could wait for it as long as anyone.

Presently they were in the hills, winding upwards, and Farnham was pointing out the landmarks of his demesne with unalloyed exuberance as they came into view. The house itself stood on its own hilltop, an old Jamaican planter's house, solidly welded to the earth and mellowed in its setting with graceful age, exposed and welcoming to the four winds. As Simon unwound himself from the car and stretched his long legs, the air he breathed in was sweet and cool.

"We're twenty-five hundred feet up," Farnham said practically. "The ideal altitude for these latitudes."

He kissed his wife as she came out to greet them, and she said: "I remember that you drank Dry Sack, Simon. And I hope you'll excuse us having dinner at sundown, but that's how we farmers live. Anyway, we're having codfish and *ackee*, which you told me you wanted to try."

"You make me feel like a prodigal son," said the Saint.

And after dinner, when he had cleaned his plate of *ackee*, that hazardous fruit which cooks up to look exactly like a dish of richly scrambled eggs, but which is deathly poison if it is plucked prematurely from the tree, he said: "And now you could sell me anywhere as a fatted calf."

They had coffee on the veranda, and made pleasant small talk for only a short while before Ellen Farnham quietly excused herself. David filled another pipe, sitting forward with his forearms on his thighs and his head bent in complete concentration on the neat performance of the job. Simon knew that now it was coming, and let him take his time.

"Well," Farnham said at last, "it just happens that you're not the only chap with a coincidence. Only a few days ago the Governor asked me to go and see the Maroons. I'd have been there already, only your wire came immediately afterwards, so I put it off till you got here."

Simon slanted a quizzical eyebrow.

"I thought you said you were all through with Government."

"I am. But the Maroons know me, and trust me, and I can talk to them. His Excellency asked me to do it as a personal favour, and I couldn't refuse."

"So I gather this trip has to be made right away."

"Tomorrow, if you don't mind."

Simon drew on his cigarette and watched smoke drift out into the velvet night.

"I'm free and willing. And it's nice of you to put off this important visit until I got here. I feel quite guilty about having kept the Maroons waiting for a cosy chat with you about the weather and the banana crop."

Farnham extinguished a match and leaned back in aromatic comfort.

"I'm sure you know the big thing we're all trying to cope with," he said soberly. "In the United States it seems to be mainly a matter of spies and fifth columnists in high places. In what's left of our poor old Empire, we have special complications. We were imperialists before the word became an international insult, and we did a pretty good job of it; but whether or not we were ever drunk with power, we're certainly getting the hangovers today. Among other things, we were left with a lot of subject people that we just jolly well conquered and took over in the days when that was a respectable thing for the white man to do. I don't think we did too badly by them, as colonialism goes, but that doesn't alter the fact that they're a readymade audience for the new propaganda against us. Well, we had to let India go. We're losing Africa piece by piece; and in the part that we really thought we could hang on to, I'm sure you've read about all that Mau Mau business. The terrorists may be natives, but you know the encouragement is Russian. And the opportunity here isn't so different."

"You don't mean you're afraid of a kind of Mau Mau outbreak in Jamaica?"

"It's already started. There have been three brutal, motiveless, barbarous killings of white people in the last six weeks."

Simon stared, frowning.

"But your coloured people aren't naked savages like the Kikuyu. They're as civilized as the Negroes in the United States."

"You'd said that about Guiana – and it wasn't so long ago, if you remember, that we had to send a warship there to nip a Communist coup in the bud. No, actually, there's a lot of difference. In some ways our coloured people are a lot better off than they are in America. There's no segregation, some of them are in big business and make a lot of money, their children go to our best schools, and they can go into any club or restaurant on the island. They not only have the vote, they hold the political power, and they're very active with it. Unfortunately some of their leaders are pretty radical. And even more unfortunately, in spite of a lot of good Government intentions there are still an enormous number who are desperately poor, totally illiterate, completely ignorant – and therefore the perfect chumps for the Communists to stir up. And that Maroon settlement makes a rather ideal focal point for it."

"I'm beginning to see a few ways that it could be used," Simon admitted slowly. "Do you know anything more about the brains of the act? – I'd hate to succumb to the obvious cliché of 'the nigger in the woodpile'."

"A little," Farnham said. "It may have started several years ago, when an English writer who's since become a rather notorious apologist for the Reds came over here and paid the Maroons a visit. Then, after a while, there were a couple of so-called artists with foreign accents who moved in with the Maroons, allegedly to paint a lot of pictures of their life and customs. I never saw the pictures, but I heard rumours that they were talking a lot of partyline poppycock to anyone who'd listen to them. But presently they went away. And then a few months ago, it seems, we got a chap we could really worry about. One of their own people."

"You mean a Russian?"

"No. A Maroon."

The Saint's brows drew lower over his quietly intent eyes.

"I see. And, of course, you're not supposed to touch him. But he'd naturally have more influence than an outsider. And if he's an upper-echelon hammer-and-sickle boy—"

"I believe he is. Our Secret Service knows a bit about him – we aren't such hopeless fuddy-duddies as some people think. There's no doubt that he's a real Maroon, but he's spent most of his life away from here. He's had a good education – and a thoroughly bad one, too. But he's got plenty of brains, and, I'm told, a terrific personality. He may be quite a problem."

Farnham got up and walked across to gaze out briefly at the stars, his old briar firmly gripped between his teeth and puffing stolidly, hands deep in his pockets, seemingly unaware of any enormity of understatement.

He said: "I don't expect you to be too concerned with our wretched colonial headaches, but a Communist base in the Caribbean would be rather nasty for all of us. Frankly, I don't quite know how I'm going to handle this blighter, and I thought if you came along you might have an idea or two."

"I'll be along, for whatever it's worth," said the Saint. Something more personal was troubling him: it was absurd, impossible within the established limits of chronology and space, but . . . "Do you know the name of this black commissar?" he asked.

"Oh, yes," Farnham said. "His background is a bit different from your Johnny's. You probably know his name. It's Mark Cuffee."

3

MR MARK CUFFEE'S career, in many respects, could have been cited as a shining example of the achievement possible to the emancipated negro, and Mr Cuffee himself had scathing epithets with which to describe those who did not regard it with unqualified admiration.

His father had left the Maroon country to work in a rum distillery soon after Mark was born, and in due course worked himself up to the rank of foreman. With visions of still higher employment in mind for his son, he sent the boy to school in Kingston, where he proved to be such a brilliant student that at seventeen he won a scholarship to Oxford. With a benevolent Sugar Industries Association supplying the necessary extra funds, he went to England, where he not only won his degree in Law with first-class honours, but also had time to represent his University both as an oarsman and a cricketer, and to give a performance in the title role of an OUDS production of *Othello* which earned such critical acclaim that he continued it professionally for a six-weeks' run in London.

After this brief triumph, knowing full well the narrow limit to the number of starring parts available to a coloured actor, no matter how talented, Mr Cuffee with apparent good philosophy turned his histrionic talents back to the Bar. He was a clever lawyer and a born virtuoso in court; and since for a while he continued to play cricket for an exclusive amateur club, he had a social entrée which in England opens all doors to distinguished adepts of the national game, provided they do not play it for money.

Thus far, his record was entirely praiseworthy, and all the auspices pointed to a successful and illustrious future.

It is not known at exactly what moment Mr Cuffee decided to turn his back on his good omens and seek other goals. One obvious milestone is the occasion when he became a Socialist candidate for Parliament in the first post-war election, and was soundly defeated in spite of the general Conservative débâcle. Others would date it from the time when a notoriously unconventional peeress, with whom the gossip had frequently linked his name, quite gracefully declined to marry him. At any rate, within a short space of both these events, he resigned from his cricket club, dropped most of his society friends, and soon afterwards went on a visit to Moscow, where he stayed for more than a year.

When he returned he wrote some articles in praise of the Soviet system for one of the pinker weeklies, and became a vitriolic public speaker against anything he could call reactionary, bourgeois, capitalist, warmongering, or, as a convenient synonym for all sins, American. Few of his former legal clients came back to him, but he was regularly retained for the defence of Communist spies and agitators, and in many other cases which could be disguised as humanitarian and used as sounding-boards for diatribes against anything that contravened the current interests of the Politburo. Although he by no means starved, he did the dirty work of his new masters and endured the inevitable public obloquy for several years, with the strange uncomplaining patience of a dedicated party member, until at last the infinitely elaborate card files in the Kremlin brought forth his name as the perfect instrument for a certain task, and he found himself back in the wild hills of Jamaica, where he had spent his boyhood.

He stood near the gate of the village of Accompong, watching a jeep bumping up the winding rocky road which the Government has built from the nearest market town to the Maroon territory, a town with the magnificent name of Maggotty. He had been watching it ever since it came in sight, having been warned of its approach by signals relayed between a chain of outposts stationed down where the farthest sentry commanded the turn-off from the main road.

Drawn up in loose formation around him were two dozen of his senior followers, whom he had been able to pick a few hours after his arrival from information supplied by previous emissaries. By now he was even more sure of them, for they were linked by what was literally a bond of blood. Most of them were clad in faded rags of incredible age, and all of these carried machetes, the all-purpose knives of the Jamaican labourer, which are as long and heavy as a cutlass and just as handy a weapon.

"Dey only two in de car," said the man nearest to him.

This was one of the few who wore presentable shirts and trousers and shoes, and in addition he had on a bandolier and a military-style peaked cap with the insigne of a gold crown fastened above the brim. Instead of a machete, he carried a large cardboard mailing tube like a staff of office.

"You didn't expect a platoon of soldiers, did you?" Cuffee said scornfully. "It'll be a long time before they dare to go that far."

He himself was dressed in riding breeches and boots, a khaki shirt with brass buttons, a Sam Browne belt, and a sun helmet painted gold and topped with a red plume. He felt slightly ridiculous in the costume, but it was traditional for the Maroon Chieftain to wear some imaginative uniform, and the inspirational effect on at least a majority of his disciples was too valuable to ignore. The pistol in the holster on his hip, however, was strictly practical and it was loaded.

The road went only as far as the gate of the settlement, and there the jeep stopped. The two men who climbed out did not look very formidable, and Cuffee could feel the rising confidence of his bodyguard as they got a closer look at them. The round-faced one with the pipe, although sturdy, was quite short; and his tall companion in the rainbow-patterned shirt was obviously a tourist. They were certainly unarmed, and even Farnham did not look at all official.

"Hullo, there," the short one called out as they approached. "May we come in?"

Cuffee stood with his thumbs hooked in his belt, aware that his ragamuffin elite guard was watching him and that much depended on his first showing.

"You're Farnham, I believe," he said.

"That's right," Farnham said, ignoring the insolent tone of the address and returning the form of it with imperturbable good humour. "And I suppose you're Cuffee."

"I'm Colonel Cuffee," was the cold reply.

In commemoration of the warrior prowess of their founding fathers, the Maroon leaders have always graded themselves by military titles, and their supreme head is 'The Colonel'. Farnham received the implied confirmation of his fears with hardly a flicker of his eyebrows.

"I'd heard rumours to that effect," he said. "Congratulations. Well, may we still come in?"

"Are you here on Government business?"

"Just a friendly visitor," Farnham said cheerfully. "Mr

Templar here is my guest on the island, and I thought he ought to have a look at the Cockpit."

"We don't want to be gaped at by tourists," Cuffee said. "And for that matter, we don't want any more uninvited visitors. There have been too many violations of our Treaty rights, and now that I'm Colonel I'm putting a stop to it."

Farnham sucked his pipe.

"Well, if that's the way you want it," he said equably, "I'll have to make it formal."

He took an envelope from his pocket and offered it across the gate. Cuffee almost put out a hand to accept it, but checked himself in time and gave a sign to his chief subordinate. The young man in the peaked cap and bandolier stepped forward and took the envelope.

"Read it aloud, Major," Cuffee said.

The letter said:

Be it known to all men by these Presents:

As Governor of Jamaica, and by virtue of the powers conferred upon me, I hereby appoint David Farnham, Esquire, my personal representative, with full authority to represent me in all matters concerning the Maroons.

Given under the Royal Seal, at Government House.

"It doesn't mean much," Farnham had confided to the Saint on the way up, "and His Excellency knows it; but it may help a bit."

The young Major read it, haltingly and with a strong native accent, with the result that some sense was clear both to the ragged men with machetes and to the Oxford-accented Colonel Cuffee.

Mr Cuffee felt reasonably confident that he could make mincemeat of any such credentials in a court of law, but he saw a pretext on which to keep face with his followers and satisfy his curiosity at the same time.

"On that basis, the free and independent Maroons will receive the Ambassador of Her Britannic Majesty – and his friend," he said. "Let them in."

Farnham ambled through the gate as it opened, looking about him with benevolent interest.

"You seem to be quite mobilized," he observed guilelessly. "I hope you aren't expecting any trouble."

"What makes you think that?" Cuffee demanded.

"I don't see any women and kids around. And the Maroons aren't usually armed."

"They've always carried machetes, Farnham. You know that perfectly well. It's just like a stockbroker with his umbrella."

"I was referring," Farnham said, "to your gun."

Cuffee's right hand touched the holster at his waist, and he laughed.

"This? Just a part of the costume. I think a sword would look better, but I couldn't find a good one at short notice."

They walked some distance up a steep rutted trail, with houses multiplying around them. A few of these could have been classed as very modest frame cottages with tarpaper roofs, more were boxlike unpainted wooden huts, and many could only be called tumbledown thatch-topped shacks. From several dark open doorways, women and children and some men looked out, but none came out or moved to join the cortège. Walking beside Farnham, as the Major walked on the far side of Cuffee, Simon could sense the unnatural tension and watchfulness that surrounded them like a dark cloud.

Presently they reached a broad grassy clearing with the habitations set back to its perimeter, which gave it something of the air of a parade ground. There Cuffee raised his hand in an imperious gesture to halt their straggling escort, and the four of them moved on a few steps and stopped again.

"All right, Farnham," Cuffee said bluntly. "What's really on your mind?"

"Well," Farnham said mildly, "the Governor thinks he should be officially informed about who is the responsible head of the Maroons."

"You know now. I'm the Colonel."

"But quite recently, we heard, they elected another Colonel. What happened to him?"

"He's gone. As soon as the community Treasury was turned over to him, he took off and hasn't been seen since."

"Dear me," Farnham said. "And nobody knows where he went?"

Cuffee shrugged.

"I don't think anyone cares very much now. The money was only a few pounds, as you can imagine, and he's probably spent it by this time. The man himself was obviously unfit for office, and we're well rid of him. There was another election, and I was elected."

"You must have made an impression very quickly," Farnham remarked. "You haven't been here long, have you?"

"I was born here. And in case you don't recognize my name, I happen to be a direct descendant of one of the first Maroon leaders, Captain Cuffee. His name is on the Treaty which still protects us."

"I know. But you're really almost a Londoner."

"It may have taken me a long time to see my duty, Farnham. But I know it now. Whatever talents I have, I inherited from my people. And the education I've gained should be used in their service."

"That's very commendable, of course."

"It's going to make a great difference, I assure you. Your Government has had everything its own way for too long. I know the policy. Keep what your Empire poet called the 'lesser breeds' in their place. Keep them downtrodden and half starved, so that they can be exploited. Keep them ignorant, so that they can be bamboozled and put upon. But you couldn't get away with it for ever. You're going to find that this is just one more place where they've got a leader at last who knows all the tricks and all the rules too. I'm going to see that every right and privilege of the Maroons is respected, in court and out of it."

Farnham nodded, pursing his lips.

"Now, about this election," he said imperturbably. "Just how was it conducted?"

"In the normal way."

"A secret ballot? With all the Maroons notified in plenty of time to assemble, and all of them casting their votes?"

Cuffee's face turned ugly and thunderous.

"That's an insulting suggestion. But I don't have to answer it, because as you're quite well aware it isn't even any of your business."

"Nevertheless, I have to ask it," Farnham persisted quietly. "And I could only put one interpretation on your refusal to answer."

Cuffee's big fist clenched and lifted a little from his side, and the Saint balanced himself imperceptibly on the balls of his feet and triggered his muscles for lightning movement; but Farnham stared up at the Colonel unblinkingly. The fist slowly lowered again, but the congestion remained in Cuffee's contorted features.

"You go too far," he said harshly. "This is exactly the kind of meddling I intend to put a stop to. I am obliged to declare you *persona non grata*. Do you know what that means?"

"In diplomatic circles, it would mean I was to be kicked out of the country."

"Precisely."

"Do you mean immediately?"

Cuffee hesitated for a second, and it was as if a mask slid over his face, smoothing out the grimace of fury and leaving only a glint of cunning in his eyes.

"No. It's late now for you to be starting back. Stay the night, if you can find a place to sleep. Let your friend look around, and make the most of it. He's the last visitor we shall admit for a long time. Since you're here, I shall give you a formal reply to take back to your Governor tomorrow. And I may also give you proof that the Maroons are behind me."

He turned on his heel and strode back towards his elite guard, his adjutant following him, leaving the Saint and David Farnham standing alone under the darkening sky.

4

"WELL," FARNHAM said stoically, "at least I think I know where we can get a bed."

The house that he led them to was one of the better ones, as evidenced by the white paint that gleamed through the dusk as they approached. Yellow lights glowed behind the windows, but the porch was dark, and on it the figure of a black man in dark clothes, standing motionless, was almost invisible until they were within speaking distance.

Farnham said affably: "Good evening, Robertson."

The man said, without moving: "Good evenin', sah."

"Aren't you going to invite us in?"

The man's shoes creaked as he shifted his weight. He said, after a pause: "No, sah. Better you go back dung de hill, sah. I' gettin' late."

"That's all right, we're not going back till tomorrow."

"Better you go tonight, sah. De Colonel don' wan' nobody from outside comin' 'ere."

"Oh, don't be ridiculous," Farnham said impatiently. "You were Colonel yourself once, the first time I came here. You know the Colonel can't stop anyone seeing his friends. And I want you to meet a friend of mine – Mr Templar."

"Yes, sah. How do you do, Mr Templar, sah? But is bes' you go dung de hill—"

The door behind him was flung open, and the shape of another man was framed in it.

"Did someone say 'Mr Templar'? Is that you, sah – the Saint?"

"Yes, Johnny," Simon said.

The man who had stood on the porch was almost bowled over in the rush as Johnny plunged past him, grabbed Simon's hand, and hustled him and Farnham into the house. Robertson followed them rather quickly, shutting the door behind them. As the lamplight revealed him, he was a very old man, and he twisted his thin gnarled fingers together feverishly.

"I don' wan' no trouble here," he mumbled.

"I don't want to make any," said the Saint. "But Johnny's the lad from New York I was telling you about, Dave."

"Pleased to meet you, Johnny," Farnham said, putting out his hand. "I've heard a lot of nice things about you."

"Colonel Robertson is a great-uncle of mine," Johnny explained. He turned to another white-haired old Negro who sat in a rocking chair in the corner. "And this is a sort of older cousin, Commander Reid."

"I've met the Commander," Farnham said, with another cordial handshake.

He sat down at the bare oilcloth-covered table and tapped the dottle from his burned-out pipe into a saucer which served as ashtray.

"And now, for heaven's sake," he said, "will one of you tell me what's got into everybody around here?"

"We don't wan' no trouble," Robertson repeated, wringing his hands mechanically.

"Goin' be lotsa change roun' here," said the Commander.

"Things are real bad, Mr Templar," Johnny said. "I found that out already. And ever since I found out, I've been wondering whether I could find you on the island, or if you'd really come here like you said you might on the plane."

"Dis Missah Templar is a fren' o' yours, Johnny?" asked the Commander, rocking busily.

Johnny looked at both the two older Negroes.

"He's a wonderful guy. In America, almost everyone knows him. He does things about people like Cuffee. If anyone can help us, he can."

"I'm just a visitor," Simon said tactfully. "Mr Farnham's the Government man."

A stout elderly woman came out of the partly screened-off kitchen and began to distribute plates laden with steaming rice and what looked like a sort of brown stew around the table. Farnham greeted her cordially as Mrs Robertson and she smiled politely and went back for more plates, without speaking, for in the councils of the older Maroons a woman's views are not asked for.

"Please, you must both eat with us," Johnny said. "And we'd be honoured to have you sleep here."

Robertson shuffled to the table and sat down, looking helpless and lonely, but the Commander pushed back his rocker and stepped across with decisive vigour.

"Okay, Johnny," he said heartily. "You' fren', and Missah

85

Farnham is my fren'. All o' we is fren'ly here. Dem help us, all okay."

The dollop of stew on the rice was made from goat, Simon decided, strongly seasoned and flavoured in part with curry. There were tough elements in it, but it was very tasty, and he discovered that his appetite had developed uncritical proportions while his mind was occupied with other things.

"You're an intelligent young man, Johnny," Farnham said across the table. "What's your version of all this nonsense?"

"It isn't nonsense, Mr Farnham, sah. This fellow Cuffee's a Communist organizer. I know. I've heard fellows up in the States who talked just like him. From what I could find out, he got himself a following pretty quick. It seems there's been some others like him here before, only white people, but talkin' the same way, so he didn't have to start out cold. But being a Maroon himself, he got a lot more attention. He had plenty of material to work with. I don't want to say anything against the Government myself, sah, I'm sure they've tried to do what they can for us, but it's a pretty hard life up here, just for a man to scratch enough from the ground to feed himself and his family. The people go down to the market an' talk to other people workin' outside, an' the young men go to Kingston an' see how there are other people no different, coloured people I mean, who are livin' so much better, an' they talk to ones who have joined the unions; an' they all come back an' talk."

"The wave of the future," Farnham said heavily. "And they want it all at once."

"Yes, sah. It takes education to be patient, an' patience to get education. An' it takes a lot of both to know why Cuffee's way won't really solve anything."

Cuffee, they learned, had organized the cadre of malcontents with swift efficiency. The disappearance of the most recently installed Colonel had provided such a fortunate vacancy that it was obviously suspect, but Johnny could only quote some of the dark rumours that had been muttered around the village of Accompong. About the handling of the latest election, however, his account was confirmed by Robertson and the Commander. Cuffee had made an inflammatory speech

86

proposing his own leadership, while his bravos shouted down the arguments of the older conservative group. Two of the most stubborn sceptics had been beaten up. Cuffee's young bullies operated the polls and announced the result.

"But they aren't an army," Farnham said. "At least, not what I saw. Can those two dozen ruffians really terrorize the whole community?"

"Hasn't the same thing happened in bigger countries, but in a not very different proportion?" Simon reminded him.

"Besides," Johnny said, "there's more than what you saw. Cuffee's got them out now, roundin' up Maroons from all over for a big meeting tomorrow, where he's goin' to tell 'em what the new system's goin' to be."

There was evidently some connection between this and Cuffee's sudden decision to let them stay overnight; and Farnham and the Saint exchanged glances.

"Just what is his platform?" Farnham asked.

"I dunno, sah. But from what I hear, I think it's something about how all the coloured people in Jamaica should have the same rights as the Maroons, an' we should let all of 'em join us who want to, and enlarge our boundaries till there's room for all of 'em."

"And eventually they end up with the whole island," Farnham said grimly. "Yes, that's clear enough." He looked suddenly very tired. "I'm afraid this turns out to be a bit out of my department. I suppose I'll just have to report it all to the Governor, and let the Government decide what to do."

"Government should be able to take care of it," Simon remarked. "A few soldiers, or even policemen—"

"You're forgetting the Treaty."

The Saint had finished his plate. He lighted a cigarette thoughtfully.

"Well, where do I stand?" he inquired. "I don't like Mr Cuffee on principle, and I didn't sign any treaty."

He was aware of a transient spark in Robertson's dull eyes and that for a moment the Commander paused in his energetic chomping, but most of all of the intent eagerness of Johnny.

"No," Farnham said firmly. "You're only a visitor. I know

your methods, and they just won't go here. This situation is ticklish enough already. Don't make it any more complicated."

"You're the boss," said the Saint; but he knew that Johnny was still looking at him.

David Farnham could not responsibly have taken any other attitude, but his enforced correctness cast an inevitable dampener over the discussion. They went to bed not long afterwards, after much repetition and no progress, and Simon sympathetically refrained from further argument when they were alone. The iron bedsteads were not luxurious, but the rough-dried sheets were fresh and clean, and the Saint never allowed vain extrapolations to interfere with his rest. A few seconds after his head settled on the pillow, he was in a dreamless sleep.

He awoke to a light touch on his shoulder instantly, without a movement or even a perceptible change in his breathing. Relaxing one eyelid just enough to give him a minimum slit to peek through, he saw Johnny's face bending over him in the first greyness of dawn, and opened both eyes.

Johnny put a finger to his lips and made a beckoning sign.

The Saint nodded, and slithered over the edge of the bed as silently as the unco-operative springs would let him. The hearty rhythm of Farnham's snoring did not change, and Johnny was already a shadow gliding through the door. A few moments later the Saint, in shirt and trousers and carrying his sandals, joined him outside.

A little way up the path from the house, in shadows made darker by the paling sky, a group of five men stood waiting. As Johnny and Simon joined them, Simon saw that Robertson and the Commander were two of them. The other three were of similar age. There were no introductions. Johnny seemed to have been appointed spokesman.

"We talked for a long time after you went to bed," he said. "I told them a lot about you. They think you might be able to help us. They want to show you the Peace Cave. That's where the Treaty is supposed to have been signed. I haven't even seen it myself. But they seem to think it's important, I don't know why. Will you go?"

"Of course," said the Saint, with a strange sensation in his spine.

T HEY SET off at once.

Nobody talked, and before long the Saint himself was grateful to be spared the effort of conversation. Even in such good condition as he always was, he was glad to save his breath for locomotion. The trail wound up innumerable steep hills and down an identical number of declivities, through arching forest and over the slippery rocks and muck of little streams. The sun came up, scorching in the open, brewing invisible steam in the deceptive shade. Simon had to marvel at the driving pace set by the Commander in the lead and uncomplainingly maintained by the other old men.

In the full light, he saw that one of them carried a bottle of rum, one carried an old oil lantern, and one had a cardboard mailing tube which was the twin of the tube that Cuffee's aide had carried. The significance of that last item puzzled him profoundly, but he managed to restrain himself from asking questions. The first rule of the whole mysterious expedition seemed to be that he should place himself blindly in their hands, and he had decided to do nothing that might upset the procedure.

They made one stop, in a grove of coconut palms. The Commander picked up a couple of fallen nuts from the ground, shook them, and threw them away. He looked up at the clusters of nuts overhead and pointed with the machete which he had carried all the way.

"Go get we some water coconut, Johnny," he said. "See if you still a good Maroon."

Johnny grinned, took off his shoes and socks, and scrambled up a tree with what Simon would have rated as remarkable agility, but which convulsed the rest of the party with good natured laughter. The Commander deftly whacked off the tops of the nuts which Johnny threw down and passed the first one to Simon.

They sat in the shade and sipped the cool mild-tasting water from the nuts, and cadged cigarettes from the Saint, but the bottle of rum was not touched. Presently the Commander stood up, flourished his machete like a cavalry officer, and led them on.

It was nearing noon when the trail turned down around a small valley and twisted past a shoulder of exposed rock and more or less massive boulders. Later, Simon was to learn that they were actually only about two miles from the village, and that the long hike had only been contrived as a kind of preliminary ordeal to test him. He could see the path winding up again beyond that, and wondered if it was ever going to reach a destination; but the Commander halted at the rocky point and the rest of the safari gathered around him.

"Now we reach de Peace Cave," said the Commander, and waved his machete. "Open de door!"

The first men to scramble up rolled aside one of the smaller stones, disclosing an opening little more than two feet square. The man with the lantern lighted it and crawled in first, on his hands and knees. Others followed. The Commander urged Simon upwards.

"Okay, Gaston," said the Saint philosophically.

The tunnel was barely large enough for him to wriggle through on all fours, but he was glad to find it only about four yards long. He squirmed out into a low vaulted cave where the lantern revealed the men who had gone ahead perched on any seats they could find on the unevenly bouldered floor. The roof was too low for him to stand up without stooping; and after Johnny and the Commander had followed him in it seemed as if the number in the party had been calculated by an instinctive sardine-packer, for it would have been almost impossible to squeeze one more adult in.

"Dis de Peace Cave," said the Commander, standing in the centre with his shoulders seeming to hold up the rock over them. "Here de Maroon dem shoot de soldiers da come after dem. Look."

He pointed back through the tunnel, and Simon saw the trail that had brought them down into the valley framed like a brilliantly lighted picture at the end of it.

"Now look down here," said the Commander.

He turned the Saint around with strong bony fingers, guiding him between two men who made way and pushing him down into a crevice at the back of the cave. There was just enough room there for a man to lie down, and at the end was a natural embrasure that looked straight up another fifty yards of the trail where it went on to climb the slope behind.

And as if he had lain there himself all those generations ago, Simon could see the soldiers in their red coats and bright equipment, probably with flags flying and bugles playing, marching in brave formation down the open path according to the manuals of gentlemanly manoeuvre of their day, sitting ducks for desperate guerillas with an instinct for taking cover and no absurd inhibitions about chivalrous warfare.

"From dere dem shoot de soldiers dat come dat way," said the Commander, as Simon clambered back out of the shallow hole. "Bang, bang!"

He made shooting pantomime, holding his machete like an imaginary musket, and roared with laughter.

"I can see why your people were never beaten," Simon said to Johnny, who had been down into the hole to look for himself.

The Commander squinted at him with shrewd bright eyes.

"You proud to be a Maroon?"

"I certainly would be. Your fathers won their freedom the hard way."

The Commander pressed him down on to a rock with a hand on his shoulder.

"Sit down," he said, and sat beside him. "Where de rum?"

The bottle was produced and opened.

"Hold out yo' hands," said the Commander.

Simon did so awkwardly, not knowing what they should be positioned for. The Commander turned them palm upwards for him and poured rum into the palms.

"Wash yo' face."

The Commander set the example, pouring rum into his own hands and rubbing it over his face and around his neck and up into his hair.

"Very good," said the Commander, beaming. "Nice, cold."

Following suit, the Saint found that it was indeed a cooling and refreshing, if somewhat odorous, substitute for cologne. The bottle passed around the circle for everyone to enjoy a similar external application. Then the Commander grabbed it and handed it to the Saint.

"Now drink."

"Skoal," said the Saint.

He took a modest sip from the bottle and passed it on. Everyone else now took an internal medication. The bottle came last to the Commander, who took a commander's swallow and firmly corked it again.

"All right," he said. "Out de light."

The cavern was suddenly plunged into blackness.

"Gimme yo' han'," said the Commander.

Simon felt fingers groping down his arm in the inky dark until they closed tightly on his wrist.

The Commander said: "Who got de knife?"

Now at last the Saint understood, and for an instant felt only the reflex drumming of his heart. It was fantastic and unreal, but he was awake and this was happening to him. He wondered fleetingly if it was only a test, a primitive elementary ordeal in darkness, and if perhaps in other days a man who flinched might have found the knife turned summarily into his heart. Intuition held him motionless, his arm relaxed. The Commander's ghoulish laugh vibrated in the cramped space.

"You have de nerve? You don' frighten?"

"Go ahead," said the Saint steadily.

"You all right," said the Commander, with respect. "Good man."

There was a tiny flick of pain at the base of the Saint's little finger, and then his hand was grasped and held as in a firm handshake and his wrist was released.

"Light de lamp," ordered the Commander.

A match flared and dimmed, and then the brighter flame of the lantern took over. The Commander still held Simon's hand, and in the renewed light the Saint saw a little trickle of blood run from between their clasped palms and drip down on the floor of the cave.

92

Five other entranced black faces leaned forward to observe the same phenomenon, and from four of them came a murmurous exhalation of approval. Johnny said: "Well, for gosh sakes."

"My blood mix wid yours," said the Commander gravely. "So A mek you mi brother. Now you is a Maroon too!" Delighted laughter shook him again as he released his grip. "Whe' de rum?"

He opened the bottle again and poured a few drops on his own wound, then on the Saint's. Then they drank again. Each of the other men solemnly shook the Saint's bloody hand, and drank from the bottle. After that the bottle was empty.

The Commander pulled out a clean handkerchief and tore it in half. He gave one half to Simon and bound the other half around his own hand.

"All right," he said. "We go back outside."

He motioned Simon to go first.

The return of sunlight was briefly blinding. While the others were climbing down from the tunnel and replacing the stone across the entrance, Simon wiped his hand and inspected the cut in it. It was reassuringly small and had already almost stopped bleeding. He fastened the cloth around it again and forgot it. Considering various aspects of the rite he had been through, a hypochrondriac would undoubtedly have been screaming for mouthwash, penicillin, and tetanus antitoxin; but the Saint had a sublime contempt for germs which may have given nervous breakdowns to innumerable hapless microbes.

He looked up and saw the Commander standing before him, with Johnny a little behind.

"Now you is a Maroon, and you is mi brother. What *you* goin' do 'bout Cuffee?"

"Well," said the Saint thoughtfully, "first of all, is there any chance of finding the other Colonel? If we produced him, at least Cuffee's election might be washed out, and we could have another."

The Commander gazed at him with bright searching eyes, and put an arm around his shoulders.

"Come."

He led the Saint only a little way off the trail, where the fast-growing jungle had already almost obliterated the traces of something heavy being dragged through it. The Saint guessed even then what he was going to see, before the sickly-sweet stench and the buzzing of disturbed flies made it a certainty, before the final pathetic travesty of swollen, glistening flesh confirmed it without need of the words which were still inevitably spoken.

"Das de Colonel," the Commander said.

6

IT WAS the Commander who had found the body, Simon learned – driven by rebellious unsatisfied curiosity, guided by atavistic senses that no civilized white man could hope to understand even if the Commander had been able to discourse professorially about them. The other elders represented there had been informed, but had been helpless to decide what should be done with the information, and afraid even to reveal their knowledge outside their own circle. The recent Colonel had been murdered, but they had no evidence to point from his body to the killer. The Commander might just as easily have been accused himself. And if the real killer had felt himself in serious jeopardy, anyone who appeared to threaten him might well be found in the same condition as the luckless ex-Colonel.

All this took some time to establish, much less concisely; and Simon could probably have deduced as much by himself more quickly, but courtesy obliged him to listen.

"It sounds just like in the States, when the gangsters knock someone off," Johnny said.

Simon nodded.

"Only here the gangster is also the Chief of Police and the Mayor too. But he can't be the Judge as well. Or is he? Don't you have any Constitution?"

They looked at him blankly, and he tried again slowly and simply.

"Is he a dictator? Can the Colonel do anything he likes?"

"De Colonel is de head man," Robertson said.

"What does the Treaty say?"

One of the others stepped forward, the man who carried the cardboard mailing tube which had puzzled the Saint intermittently since the day before. He held it out.

"See de Treaty yah, sah."

The Saint took it and stared at it. It gave him a strange feeling to be holding that much-discussed document at last, after all he had heard about it. It seemed extraordinary, now, that this moment had been so long delayed; and yet he had not realized before what an essential element had been lacking.

"Well I'm damned," he said; and then another thought rebounded. "Where did you get this copy?"

"De new Major is mi gran'son, sah. Him is a very wil' bwoy. Him keep it fe Cuffee. A tek it las' night while him was sleepin'."

Simon carried it to a convenient rock and sat down. He lighted a cigarette, and then carefully extracted the scroll from the tube and as carefully unrolled it. Johnny had followed him, and was peering over his shoulder.

The parchment was yellowed and stained with age and the antique angular script often hard to decipher. But the following is an exact transcription; and if there are any sceptics who still doubt the authenticity of these chronicles, I should like to say that they can see the original in Kingston whenever they care to go there. I make no apology for quoting it at such length, for it is a real historical curiosity.

At the Camp near
Trelawny Town
March 1st 1738

In the name of God Amen.

Whereas Captain Cudjoe, Captain Accompong, Captain Johnny, Captain Cuffee, Captain Quaco, and several other Negroes their dependants and adherents, have been in a state of war and hostility for several years past against our Sovereign Lord the King and the inhabitants of this Island; and whereas peace and friendship among mankind and the preventing the

95

*effusion of blood is agreeable to God consonant to reason and
desired by every good man; and whereas his Majesty George
the Second, King of Great Britain, France and Ireland and of
Jamaica, Lord &c. has*

"King of France too?" said the Saint. "That's a new one
on me."

*has by his letters patent dated February 25th 1738 in the
twelfth year of his reign granted full power and authority to
John Guthrie and Francis Sadler, Esquires, to negotiate and
finally conclude a treaty of peace and friendship with the afore-
said Captain Cudjoe, the rest of his captains adherents and his
men; they mutually, sincerely and amicably have agreed to the
following Articles:*

1st. That all hostilities shall cease on both sides for ever.

*2nd. That the said Captain Cudjoe, the rest of his Cap-
tains, adherents and men shall be for ever hereafter in a perfect
state of freedom and liberty, excepting those who have been
taken by them or fled to them within two years last past if such
are willing to return to their said masters and owners with full
pardon and indemnity from their said masters or owners for
what is past; provided always that if they are not willing to
return they shall remain in subjection to Captain Cudjoe and
in friendship with us according to the form and tenor of this
treaty.*

*3rd. That they shall enjoy and possess for themselves and
posterity for ever, all the lands situate and lying between Trelawny Town and the Cockpits to the amount of 1500 acres
bearing north west from the said Trelawny Town.*

There followed paragraphs defining the rights of farming,
marketing, and hunting, and binding the Maroons to join the
Governor in suppressing other rebels or repelling foreign
invaders. Then:

*8th That if any white man shall do any manner of injury
to Captain Cudjoe, his successors, or any of his or their people*

they shall apply to any commanding officer or Magistrate in the neighbourhood for justice and in case Captain Cudjoe or any of his people shall do any injury to any white person he shall submit himself or deliver up such offenders to justice.

9th   That if any Negroes shall hereafter run away from their master or owners and fall into Captain Cudjoe's hands they shall immediately be sent back to the Chief Magistrate of the next parish where they are taken; and those that bring them are to be satisfied for their trouble as the legislature shall appoint.

10th.   That all Negroes taken since the raising of this party by Captain Cudjoe's people shall immediately be returned.

"That seems to settle Cuffee's idea of taking all the other coloured people in Jamaica into the Maroons," Simon remarked.

"But they aren't slaves any longer," Johnny said. "So how could they be returned?"

"It'll give the lawyers something to haggle with, anyway," said the Saint. "But Cuffee's a lawyer himself. I'm looking for some law we can use now."

11th.   That Captain Cudjoe and his successors, shall wait on His Excellency or the commander in chief for the time being once every year if thereto required.

"And that's a big help."

12th.   That Captain Cudjoe during his life, and the Captains succeeding him shall have full power to inflict any punishment they think proper for crimes committed by their men among themselves, death only excepted; in which case, if the Captain thinks they deserve death he shall be obliged to bring them before any Justice of the Peace, who shall order proceedings on their trial equal to those of other free Negroes.

13th.   That Captain Cudjoe and his people shall cut, clear and keep open large and convenient roads—

"God burn it," said the Saint in disgust, "it just starts to get somewhere and then it veers off again. And there are only a few lines left."

*14th. That two white men to be nominated by His Ex-
cellency or the commander in chief for the time being shall
constantly live and reside with Captain Cudjoe and his successors in order to maintain a friendly correspondence with
the inhabitants of this Island.*

"That's an item that somebody seems to have overlooked,"
Simon observed. "It might be some help, but it isn't exactly a
lightning solution."

The excitement with which he had started reading was beginning to drag its tail. The lift of a couple of false hopes had
only made the subsequent letdowns more discouraging. The
Treaty, although its simplicity and straightforwardness could
have been studied with advantage by the architects of more
modern pacts, left vast areas untouched. The only regulation it
set up for the internal affairs of the Maroons was that they
should not execute each other. How otherwise they should
organize their freedom seemed to have been wholly outside the
scope of the agenda.

There was only one clause left; and the Saint's heart sank as
the first words foreshadowed its stately irrelevance.

*15th. That Captain Cudjoe shall during his life, be Chief
Commander in Trelawny Town; after his decease the command
to devolve on his brother Captain Accompong, and in case of
his decease to his next brother Captain Johnny; and failing
him, Captain Cuffee shall succeed; who is to be succeeded by
Captain Quaco—*

His eyes widened incredulously over the next three and final
lines.

He read them again to make sure.

His pointing forefinger underlined them slowly, and he
looked up to meet the stunned stare of Johnny at his shoulder.

"You see what I see, don't you?" said the Saint.

"Yes, sah. But—"

"Oh, no," said the Saint in a low quavering voice. "Oh,
leaping lizards. Oh, holy Moses in the mountains!"

He was rolling the parchment up again with shaking fingers,

98

stuffing it back into the protective tube. He came to his feet with a shout that brought all the others around him.

"O blessed bureaucracy," he yelled. "O divine dust of departmental archives. O rollicking ribbons of red tape!"

They gaped at him as if he had gone out of his mind, which perhaps he temporarily had. The immortal magnificence of that moment was more than flesh and blood could take with equanimity. And it was all crystallized in the last few words of the Maroons' charter, after he had given up all hope – exactly like a charge of cavalry pounding to the rescue of a beleaguered outpost in the last few feet of the corniest horse opera ever filmed.

Simon's ribs ached with laughter. He handed the tube back to the man who had carried it, and clapped Johnny and the Commander ecstatically on the back, one with each hand.

"Let's get back to Accompong," he said. "And somebody better find something we can eat on the way. This is going to be a day to remember, and I don't want to starve to death before I see the end of it."

7

"I'VE TOLD you till I'm blue in the face," David Farnham said irritably. "I don't know where Mr Templar went, or why, or anything about it."

It was late in the afternoon, and he must have repeated the same statement twenty or thirty times during the day. It was unequivocally true; for Mrs Robertson, who had served him breakfast and a sandwich for lunch, had been blandly unable to enlighten him on that subject, or on the whereabouts of her husband, or the Commander, or Johnny. Farnham was considerably perplexed, but not too worried, for the attitudes of Cuffee and his henchmen clearly proved that they were equally baffled by the disappearance.

Cuffee scowled. The Major, zealously taking his cue, scowled even more ferociously. Others of the bodyguard dutifully joined in the glowering.

They were in a house at the edge of the 'parade-ground'

where Cuffee was living and making his official headquarters. Twenty yards in front of it, men had been working all day to build a sort of open bandstand about fifteen feet square, with a floor raised two feet above the ground and stout poles at each corner supporting a thatched roof. Now it was completed; and for the past hour the wide clearing had been gradually filling with a motley crowd of men, drifting and conglomerating and separating again uncertainly, with chattering groups of women on its outskirts and small children chasing each other like puppies around its fringes. Several of Cuffee's elite corps were trying to marshal the mob into a semblance of audience formation facing the newly erected platform. They were now distinguished with broad red armbands, which seemed to give them the added confidence and bravado of a uniform.

Cuffee looked at his watch. He was restless. Although he knew that schedules meant little to the Maroons, he had set a time for himself; and even more importantly, he sensed that if the suspense of the people waiting to hear him were prolonged beyond a certain point it might have the opposite effect from what he wanted.

With an abrupt decisiveness he stood up, settled his Sam Browne belt, and put on his gilded helmet.

"The meeting will begin," he said, and looked at Farnham. "I think you'll want to listen to this."

"I shall be very interested," Farnham said calmly.

Cuffee turned and marched out, followed by his adjutant and the rest of his bodyguard, except for two who remained with Farnham.

Farnham strolled out, relighting his pipe, and the two followed him. Cuffee had not invited him to join him on the rostrum, and Farnham wondered whether he should take the invitation for granted or the lack of it as a diplomatic affront. His two personal escorts, however, who seemed to have received prior instructions, fell in on either side of him and steered him with suggestive pressures around the reviewing stand to a place close in front of it and in line with one corner, where he discovered that an empty wooden crate had been placed on which it was indicated that he should sit. Thus he found himself nearer the platform than the nearest of the other spectators, but set aside rather than in the centre of a special front row. It gave him an uncomfortable feeling of being positioned more like a prisoner on trial which was not relieved by the way his escorts stationed themselves just behind him, one on each side with their machetes in hand. But he decided that his best course was to appear unaware of anything out of the ordinary unless and until it was forced upon him, and he crossed his legs composedly and tried to look as if he felt that he was only being treated with proper deference.

A dozen of the elite guard had ranged themselves in a double rank from front to rear of the dais, with the Major in the front of one file. At a word from him, they raised their clenched fists in a ragged salute, and Cuffee strode down the human aisle to the front of the stand, where he raised his fist in salute to the audience.

There was a splatter of applause, which Farnham observed was led and fomented by a number of the red-armleted who still circulated authoritatively through the assembly.

Cuffee lowered his fist, and his guard of honour slouched out of formation and shuffled towards the front of the stage.

"My friends," Cuffee said, "comrades, and brother Maroons, I am your new Colonel. Colonel Cuffee. I've brought you here to meet me, and to let me tell you what I'm going to do for you, and for all our people, while I'm your leader."

His oratorical voice was resonant and dynamic, and he handled it with the skill of an actor. But with even greater intellectual skill he chose words of almost puerile simplicity but uttered them with overwhelming earnestness, investing them with vast profundity, never seeming to talk down to his listeners, yet contriving to make sure that the most ignorant and unschooled of them could scarcely fail to grasp his meaning.

He started harmlessly enough with a short recital of their history, reminding them of how their ancestors had been torn from their African homes and brought to Jamaica like cattle to make a few white capitalists richer, of how they had rebelled against abuse and slavery, of how they had fought for their freedom against the might of the whole British Empire and forced the King of England himself to plead for peace, and of how the Treaty had finally recognized their right to hold the lands they had defended and to be free for ever of any outside domination.

So far it was not much worse than any nation's jingoistic version of its own trials and triumphs, although plainly slanted to revive ancient resentments and hint at villains yet to receive their just punishments; but Mark Cuffee was still only laying his groundwork.

"It is a pity," he said, "that the spirit of our Treaty was soon forgotten by the Government of this island. The English Kings had been made to feel small, and they didn't like that. They couldn't wipe out the Treaty, but they could try to make it mean less and less. And because some of our fathers were not wide awake, or were deceived by tricks and lies, they let their rights be taken away one by one."

He cited an insidiously increasing variety of encroachments. Their lands had never been properly surveyed, and their boundaries had been involved in a continual series of disputes designed to whittle them away acre by acre. Their own administration of their own affairs had been spied on and meddled with by a procession of imperialist agents disguised as missionaries or welfare workers. Their territory had been arrogantly invaded by British policemen with instructions to fabricate evidence that the Maroons were bandits or were harbouring bandits; their privilege of self-government was nullified by emissaries of the Colonial Secretariat who presumed to force their way in and ask impertinent questions about their manner of conducting elections and to cast doubt on their validity.

It was during the development of this theme that Cuffee began to turn pointed glances towards David Farnham, and the last charge was pointed straight at him.

"Nonsense!" Farnham said loudly; but he felt the impact of hostile stares and heard some ugly muttering in the audience.

Also he had a mostly psychic impression of his two special guards stiffening and hefting their machetes when he spoke, and for the first time felt a real qualm of somewhat incredulous apprehension.

Where the devil had the Saint gone? he wondered.

He recrossed his legs and moved his pipe to the other side of his mouth with a good show of phlegmatic ennui as Cuffee turned away from him again with calculated contempt and made another smooth shift from second into high gear.

"But, comrades, we don't have to let them do this. Now I shall tell you what we can do – what we are going to do."

The only thing wrong with the Treaty was that it had not gone far enough. The Maroons had won their freedom, but for many years after that their fellow slaves had been kept in bondage. Even when they were finally set free, they had not been compensated with lands for the initial crime committed against them. They still had no true independence. Even though today they could vote, they could vote only for British governments. They were still subjects of the same flag that had flown over the slave ships.

"Now I say that it is time for us to set another glorious example. Let us urge our comrades outside to demand the same rights that we have. Let us help them to get their rights. Let us tell any of them who want to fight for their rights, that if the British tyrants want to put them in jail for it, they can come here, where they'll be safe, because the British police can't come to our country to arrest them—"

Farnham could sit still no longer. He jumped to his feet.

"That's treason!" he shouted.

"Also," said another voice, "it's against the Treaty."

The voice turned every eye, before any move could develop against Farnham. And everyone saw the Saint, with the little group of Johnny and the old men behind him, standing at the other corner of the rostrum.

The Commander stepped forward and held up the Saint's hand with his own, so that their two bandages were together in plain sight.

"Dis man is mi brother!" he roared. "Him is a good Maroon now. A good man. Oono listen to him!"

The bloodstains on the cloth stood out so clearly that the

delicate pink flush of evening that was touching the tops of the clouds looked like a pale reflection from them; and an awed murmur rippled through the crowd and settled into a complete hush.

"In our Treaty," said the Saint, "the Maroons promised to help stop rebellions, not start them."

The man who carried the cardboard tube held it up symbolically.

The young Major's eyes blazed as he saw it. He leaped down from the stand, snatched the tube away, and felled the old man with a brutal blow. In another second he measured more than his own length on the ground, sliding on his back, as Johnny connected with a classic straight left to his chin.

Simon grabbed the tube as it fell and sprang up on the platform. Johnny was close behind him; and David Farnham had started in the same direction before his guards could recover from their astonishment and stop him. Farnham's move was made without conscious thought, but it seemed inevitable that all hell would break loose in a moment, and although the end could only be disastrous he felt that he should be at the core of it.

The swift succession of surprises, however, seemed to have temporarily robbed everyone else of initiative. Even the red-armbanded squad on the platform were as nonplussed as their colleagues among the crowd: still too new to their rôle to have developed the reflexes of trained and organized bullies, they waited uncertainly for orders, and for a moment Cuffee himself hesitated before the fateful possibilities of his decision.

In that breathing spell of confusion, Simon Templar raised and stretched out his arms to the audience, with the tube held aloft in one of them, and said:

"I shall not stop Colonel Cuffee talking for long – although I should only call him Captain Cuffee, because I see in the Treaty that the Maroons who set you all free were none of them more than Captains, and I don't know why anyone today should make himself bigger than those men who signed this Treaty. I have it here, and I have read it. All of you should read it. It has not been read enough. For years people have talked about this Treaty, here and in the Government too; but I think very few of them have ever looked at it. If they had, there would not be so many arguments. For instance, about your – our last election, in which Captain Cuffee made himself the chief. You should all know what the Treaty says!"

He thrust the tube into Farnham's hands, and said: "Read 'em the last clause – and try not to look shocked yourself."

Cuffee started to move then, but in the same instant Johnny pinioned his arms from behind. In the next, Simon had whipped the gun out of Cuffee's holster and levelled it.

"Tell your boys to stand back," he said grimly. "Because if a riot starts now, you'll be the first casualty."

As Johnny released him and stepped warily away, Cuffee made a perfunctory gesture of compliance. It was almost supererogatory, for the sight of the gun had already cooled the ambition of his cohorts.

Farnham held the unrolled parchment, and read with pedagogic clarity:

"'That Captain Cudjoe shall during his life, be Chief Commander in Trelawny Town; after his decease the command to devolve on his brother Captain Accompong, and in case of his decease to his next brother Captain Johnny; and failing him Captain Cuffee shall succeed; who is to be succeeded by Captain Quaco; and after all their demises . . .'" His voice faltered as his eyes ran ahead of it, but he braced himself and finished strongly and firmly: "'. . . and after all their demises the Governor or Commander-in-Chief for the time being shall appoint from time to time, whom he thinks fit for that command.'"

There was a silence in which the earth itself seemed to stand still, and then it was as if all the people breathed together in a great sigh.

Farnham let the scroll curl up again.

"As the official representative of the Governor, therefore," he said, "I declare that Cuffee is no longer your Colonel."

There was a vague medley of gasps and murmurs in the audience, and several sporadic handclaps.

Farnham looked at the Saint, and Simon nodded and put a

hand on Johnny's shoulder. Farnham turned again to the assembly.

"Instead, I shall appoint another man who has been to school and learned a lot of things that will help you, but who's also a good Maroon, whose ancestor is named in the Treaty even ahead of Cuffee's – Captain Johnny!"

Simon seized Johnny's hand and hoisted it like the mitt of a victorious prize fighter.

The murmurs became more positively approving, the applause louder; and the Commander started a gleeful cheer which was taken up by an increasing number of voices.

Cuffee's face was grey under its dusky pigment. Ignoring the gun that the Saint held, in sudden desperation, he forced his way again to the front of the platform, his clenched fist raised.

"That's what I've been telling you!" he howled. "The Treaty cheated you! You're still slaves—"

Johnny spun him around by the shoulder and flung him into the arms of the nearest of his own men.

"Arrest him," he said.

It was as if an invisible mantle had fallen upon him that had always been waiting for him to find his own stature, the stature that it was made for. The tone of command came without effort to his voice.

The men glanced nervously about them, and must have heard in the rising babble of the crowd beyond a trend that would not lightly change its course again. Already some of their fraternity in the audience were unobtrusively slipping off their red armlets. . . . They took hold of Cuffee and held him, instinctively obeying the one who seemed to be the stronger leader.

Johnny turned back to the throng that was crowding up to the dais.

"That man lied to you about the Treaty!" he shouted. "Why should we listen to him any more? He lied about the last Colonel, too. Cuffee killed him so that he could make himself Colonel. We found his body near the Peace Cave. The Commander saw it too, an' Colonel Robertson, an' Mr Templar."

Of course it was not evidence, but to his hearers it carried conviction. An appalled hush settled again.

"Nobody does himself any good by breakin' the law," Johnny said with simple dignity. "The Treaty is our law. An' it's a good Treaty. Whatever the British Government did once, they want to be our friends now. It isn't anything like Cuffee tried to make out. If you'll listen, an' Mr Farnham will help me, I'll try to tell you why."

8

LATER THAT evening Farnham said meticulously: "Of course, Johnny, between ourselves, the Governor'll have to approve my recommendation and confirm your appointment himself. But I don't think we'll have any trouble about that. He should be grateful to have such a tidy solution dropped into his lap. . . . As for you, Simon, I think I'd feel better if you went ahead and laughed at me, instead of displaying such hypocritical Christian forbearance."

"Because you'd never read the Treaty right to the end yourself?" said the Saint. "No, I did most of my laughing this morning, and not principally at you. Hereafter we'll keep the joke to ourselves. Besides which, I doubt if anyone else would ever believe it."

He lighted a cigarette and shook his head in rapture nevertheless.

"But what a fabulous little gem it is," he said dreamily. "For more than two hundred years the legend of the Maroons has gone on. Away back somewhere, some clerk in whatever Government department it would be told some new clerk who was too lazy to look for himself his careless version of what the Treaty said. That clerk repeated it to his successor, who repeated it to the next man. Everyone accepted it and believed it. Each new incoming Governor heard about it from his staff, believed it, and perpetuated it. It was such general knowledge that nobody ever thought of questioning it, any more than they would have questioned the statement that Jamaica is a British colony. Jerry Dugdale, the policeman, believed it, and so did the Governor who bawled him out. You believed it. A copy of the Treaty was in the files all the time, but who ever looks in files? For maybe two centuries, *nobody ever read the Treaty.* Except probably Cuffee. But why should he blow his hand? It took a nosy parker like me, sitting on a rock out in the wilderness, to read all through the damn thing and explode the lovely myth."

"All right," Farnham said stolidly. "There's only one thing that bothers me now. It's about Cuffee. None of us has any reasonable doubt that he murdered the former Colonel – or if he didn't do it himself, he instigated it. But the Treaty doesn't allow you to hang him, Johnny. You have to hand him over to our authorities. And there's no evidence against him that would stand up in a regular court. I'm very much afraid that he'll eventually get off scotfree."

The Saint stood up.

"I've been thinking about that myself," he added soberly. "And I have an idea. But if you'll excuse me, I'd rather tell Johnny alone. If you know nothing about it, you can't have anything on your conscience."

Mr Mark Cuffee had been gradually regaining his confidence as he endlessly paced the confines of the room that had become his cell. The men who guarded him now were half a dozen of the older generation, headed by the Commander, and he knew that it would have been a waste of breath to try to argue or coax them into changing their allegiance. Nor had he been foolish enough to attempt a forcible escape: in spite of their years, they still had the sinews of a lifetime of manual labour, and any two of them would have been an easy match for him. So instead of attempting the impossible, he had been using his head.

There was no evidence that could possibly convict him in a British court. And with his knowledge and experience as a barrister, he would back himself to make any colonial prosecutor in that little island look like a clown. There were even opportunities for such a grandstand performance that his superiors in the party, of whom he was much more afraid, might not only forgive his local failure but commend the larger achievement. His defence of himself and his struggle to liberate a downtrodden proletariat from imperialist exploiters would make worldwide headlines. He would—

As the door opened and Johnny and Simon Templar walked in, he swung around as if he himself were the potential prosecutor and they must have come to plead for leniency.

"What do you want now?" he challenged truculently. "I demand to be properly arraigned before a magistrate. Until you're ready to conform with civilized legal procedures, be good enough to leave me alone."

"That's what I wanted to talk to you about," said the Saint quietly. Johnny made a sign to the guard, and one by one they silently left the room. As the door closed behind the last of them, Cuffee threw himself into a chair.

"What's the idea?" he inquired sarcastically. "Were you thinking of trying some American third degree on me? It won't get you anywhere, and it'll only make matters worse for you when I get you in court."

"Mr Cuffee," said the Saint, "you aren't going to any court where you'd probably get acquitted. Johnny has decided that it would be better for him to convict you on a lesser charge, and give you a sentence which he has the right to impose. You remember that the Treaty allows him to inflict any punishment short of death. Therefore his idea is that he should have your hands and feet cut off, your eyes put out, your tongue cut out, castrate you – and let you go."

Cuffee stared at them.

"You must be crazy," he sneered. "I shall appeal to the Governor—"

"The sentence is to be carried out tonight."

Cuffee licked his lips. He could not believe his ears, but Johnny's face was expressionless and implacable. And something in Cuffee's own cosmogony, harking back to a primitive heritage which at any other time he would have been the first to deride, made him believe that a man of his own race could well be capable of such savagery.

"You're off your head, Johnny," he said in a husky mumble

of horror. "England would never let you get away with that, Treaty or no Treaty. You'd pay for it in the end, you and all the Maroons."

"That's what I've tried to tell him," said the Saint. "But he won't listen. His mind's made up. And by the time the British Parliament could do anything about it, it'll be too late to do you any good. The best I've been able to do is persuade him to let you take an easier way out for yourself, if you want to."

He brought one hand from behind his back, and Cuffee saw that there was a coiled length of rope in it. Cuffee gazed at it numbly as the Saint laid it across his knees.

"It's a strong rope," said the Saint, "and so are the beams over your head. You'll be left alone for half an hour before they come for you. I'm sorry, but that's all I could do."

He turned and walked out of the room; and Johnny followed him, closing the door after them.

They stood in front of the house, under the stars, looking at the fires that had been lighted on the parade ground and hearing the voices of the Maroons who, having been brought together anyway, had decided with typical good spirits to make their convening an excuse for a feast and celebration. Excited chattering voices which, to a guilty man, could easily sound like the ominous hysteria of a sadistic mob. . . .

"You know, sah," Johnny said, "I happened to see an old map of Jamaica in Kingston, an' I saw what they used to call this part of the country. You know what it was? *The District of Look Behind.* I kept rememberin' that when we were at the Peace Cave, thinkin' how they used to ambush the redcoats. Kind of gives you a shudder, doesn't it?"

"My God, what a wonderful name," said the Saint, with the pure delight of a poet. Then his hand lay on Johnny's shoulder, and he said: "But now it's your job to make it the District of Look Ahead."

Then they both looked back at the house, and listened.

— PUERTO RICO —

THE UNKIND PHILANTHROPIST

"ONE OF these days," said Simon Templar lazily, "when I decide to become Dictator of the Universe, I shall issue a law for the protection of men's names. This modern fad of giving them to girls has got to be stopped somewhere. It was bad enough when women broke out in a rash of semi-masculine diminutives, occasionally with and just as often without some connection with the monickers they got baptized with, of which I have known for instance, Bobbie, Billie, Jo, Charlie, Marty, Jacky, Jerry, Freddie, Tommy, Dickie, Stevie, Teddy, Tony—"

"Braggart," said Tristan Brown.

"After which," Simon continued inexorably, "I have seen the movie marquees blossom with actresses calling themselves, with or without baptismal authority, by such traditionally male labels as Toby, Dale, Gene, Jeff, Robin, Gregg, Terry, Alexis, and heaven knows what next. In my own limited acquaintance of females, I can vouch for dolls who were actually christened Franklin, Craig, Cameron, Christopher, and even George."

"How about the men I've known," Tristan inquired, "who were called Jess, Evelyn and Shirley?"

"I think a little research would show that they had the prior claim. Only they lost it sooner. Like that guy who keeps on writing about me. He's always getting circulars from mail-order lingerie merchants addressed to Miss Leslie Charteris. It's getting so that about the only name you could give your son today, with reasonable certainty that no women would be wearing it tomorrow, would be something like Gladys."

"I think Tristan is a nice name," she said tartly. "So did my father. Brown is dull enough for a surname, so he tried to liven it up. I like it."

Simon squeezed the car past a crawling truck topheavy with sugar cane.

"I'm the old-fashioned type," he said gloomily. "I think girls should have girls' names. If you ever suffered through the opera, you'd remember that Tristan was a man."

"What does the name of Morgan make you think of?" she asked.

"J. P. Morgan. A big business man. Or before him, Sir Henry Morgan – another very male go-getter, in his way."

"But in the same legend that Tristan came from, wasn't Morgan le Fay a woman?"

Just for a moment Simon was stopped.

"Well, as I recall it, she was the queen of the fairies," he said, and the girl had to laugh.

It was merely an idle conversation to lighten the drive from San Juan up into the mountains of Puerto Rico, and the Saint had no idea at the time of the significance that the thought behind it would have in his always unpredictable odyssey.

Tristan Brown had entered his life during his first morning on the island, on a tour of the historic fortress of El Morro, which dominates the narrow entrance of the spacious harbour which Christopher Columbus discovered, and whence later Ponce de León, then Governor of the colony, sailed on his famous quest for the Fountain of Youth which took him only to Florida and his death. And because she was very noticeably feminine, in spite of the name which he had yet to find out, with urchin-cut mahogany hair and eager brown eyes and a figure that moulded exactly the right curves into a thin cotton dress, and in fact would have been an exciting person to see even in a much less nondescript crowd, Simon automatically manoeuvred himself next to her as the party moved along and thoughtfully contrived to stay there.

The guide was explaining with the aid of a map how Puerto Rico's strategic position had once made it the natural rendezvous for the Spanish treasure convoys that fanned out on their golden quests all up and down the coasts of Central and South America, and how for the same reason it was coveted by the privateers who cruised the Caribbean to loot the looters on their homeward voyage; and she saw the Saint and could not help thinking how much like the idealized conception of a pirate he looked, with the trade wind ruffling his dark hair and the sun on his keen tanned face and a half smile on his strong, reckless mouth. Against those battlements the tall swordsman's grace of his body and the merry insolence of his blue eyes seemed to span the centuries as easily as the weathered stone, so that with the slightest imagined change of costume she could see him as the living prototype of what the heroes of innumerable Technicolor movies tried ineffectually to re-create; but with him she had a strange disturbing feeling that the resemblance was real. . . . And she awoke to the awareness that she was still staring at him, and that he knew it.

Farther along, someone asked: "Was this fort ever captured?"

"Not until the Spanish–American War," said the conductor, with some pride. "And then it was mostly by invitation. The English and the Dutch tried to take it for a couple of hundred years, but they weren't good enough. In 1595, they even gave the great Sir Francis Drake a licking."

"And I bet you won't find that in an English history book," Simon murmured to the girl.

By that time she had recovered from her confusion.

"Who was it said that histories are always written by the winning side?" she responded easily.

"I don't know, but it's probably true. Drake must have been pretty young then, and he did get his own back on the Armada. But he'd be a still bigger man if they didn't try to make him look like a winner all the time."

After that, when the tour was over and she asked directions back from the castle, it was easy to offer his personal guiding service, and he walked her by way of the Fortaleza up into the narrow streets of the old town. Then it was time for lunch, and the restaurant El Mesôn was conveniently near by.

Over glasses of Dry Sack they exchanged names, and she recognized his at once.

"I just knew it would have to be something like that when I first saw you," she said, but she declined to explain what she meant.

"To answer the routine question you're dying to ask," he said, "I'm not in the midst of any felonious business. I'm just island-hopping and amusing myself."

"Spending your ill-gotten gains?"

"Maybe."

"And I'm spending somebody else's," she said brightly.

"Does he know about it?"

"Oh, no. He's dead." She laughed at the restrained lift of his brows, and said: "Have you heard of the Ogden H. Kiel Foundation?"

"Of course?"

For the benefit of any unlikely person who may not have heard of it, it may be recalled that Mr Ogden H. Keil was a shining example of free enterprise who, starting away back with a bottle of snake oil and a medicine show, parlayed himself into a patent medicine empire that loaded the drugstore shelves of the nation with an assortment of salves, lotions, potions, physics, and vitamin compounds which, if all their various claims could be believed, should have banished every human ailment from the face of this planet. The fact that this millennium did not supervene must have spurred him to continually more frenzied efforts of distribution, through the media of printed advertising, radio, and television, so that the sale of his nostrums brought him a flood of wealth which not even modern taxes could reduce to a stream of a size that even a lavish liver could spend. Wherefore he had created the Ogden H. Kiel Foundation, dedicated (to do him justice) to giving suffering humanity more substantial forms of relief than gaily coloured pills – an institution which, upon probate of his will, found itself with more than eighty million dollars in the kitty and at least another million in royalties accruing every year.

"I work for it," Tristan Brown said. "For a mere hundred dollars a week, plus my expenses, I help to give away millions."

"How does one get a job like that?" Simon inquired with interest.

"I happen to be a lawyer. Don't look indignant – it's quite legal! The firm of which I'm a very junior member happens to be the trustees of the fund. It takes six of us all our time to get around and find places to leave cheques. It isn't half the life you'd think it would be, but I'm seeing a lot of the world."

"And you're here to hand out some of this dough in Puerto Rico?"

"It's the kind of territory that the Foundation is set up to help, and I'm supposed to find the best channel for one of our grants."

"How about me? A million dollars would rehabilitate me right out of sight."

"That's what I'd be afraid of," she said dryly.

He sighed.

"It's prejudices like that," he said, "that have forced me into my life of crime."

He introduced her to *ompanadas*, succulent pasties filled with a mixture of ground meat, almonds, raisins, olives, and capers, and *mofongo*, a fried mash of green plantains mixed with cracklings, garlic, coriander, and cayenne; and she made him talk more about himself. She made it easy for him to do, revealing a most unlawyerlike delight in the motives and methods which had made the Saint almost as mythological a figure as the Robin Hood with whom he was always inevitably compared. And since there was nothing mythical at all about his reaction to any beautiful girl, it must be admitted that he thoroughly enjoyed the realization that her response to him as a person was much warmer than the basic requirements of intellectual research.

But the Saint was also an extraordinarily careful man in some ways, and a pretty girl who claimed to be a qualified attorney and moreover to be entrusted with such a fantastic responsibility as Tristan Brown was a sufficiently unusual phenomenon to draw a delicate screen of caution between his intelligence and his impulses.

Everything she said might be perfectly true. But just as possibly, everything she said might be only the groundwork for some bunko routine that would presently begin to take a familiar shape.

The Saint was no stranger to the technique of the Colossal Lie. He had used it himself, on occasion. If you say you are the sheriff of some unheard-of county in Texas, almost any reasonably suspicious citizen will check up on you. But if you say you are a Governor of the Bank of England, and pick up a telephone and invite anyone to call London and verify it, the average sucker will figure that nobody would dare to tell such a preposterous tale if his bluff could be called so easily, and will not even bother to put it to the test.

Simon permitted himself to keep a pleasantly open mind about Tristan Brown. But he also permitted himself to lead her into telling him that she had graduated from Columbia Law School, and as soon as he was back at his hotel he looked up the address of the Ogden H. Kiel Foundation in a New York directory; and that same afternoon he sent off two telegrams.

While he waited for the replies, however, there was nothing to stop him getting the maximum pleasure out of their acquaintance. He took her to dinner at the Casino, danced and played harmless roulette with her at Jack's, and was making more plans for the next day as he strolled back with her to their hotel.

"I have to work tomorrow," she said firmly. "I'm visiting the Guavate prison camp. They're sending a car for me."

"Tell 'em you'll get there on your own," he said. "Let me rent a car and drive you up. I'll wait for you, and we can come back by way of El Yunque, which you ought to see."

That was how he came to be driving her up the narrow winding road out of Caguas, making trivial banter about the male and female names.

They turned into the Guavate National Forest and went on twisting upwards, glimpsing simple vacation cabins and rocky streams tumbling between the trees, and then out of the deepest shade and still winding upwards along steep slopes green with banana trees and opening on to vast, blue-veiled panoramas of the lower hills, and so at last to a wide open gateway across the road where a guard was negligently taking a light for his cigarette from one of a group of convicts. Beyond, there were plain clean-looking buildings without bars or wire, and many more brown-skinned men in prison denims who worked or loafed and turned to stare at them with uninhibited and amiable curiosity.

"Don't apologize for not asking me in," said the Saint. "Something about me is allergic to prisons, even when they have a lovely setting like this. I'll have lunch in Caguas and come back for you about three."

And that was how he happened to meet Mr Elmer Quire.

2

Mr Quire was a stout man with a ruddy face and a shock of white hair, a thin beak of a nose, and bright eyes that twinkled behind heavy black spectacle frames, so that he looked rather like an elderly and benevolent owl. He had a slight tic which kept his head nodding almost imperceptibly, a movement which in combination with his bluff paternal manner made him seem ingratiatingly sympathetic and co-operative to anyone who was talking to him. It was an affliction that had proved to be anything but a disadvantage to him in his operations.

He was ready to tell anyone who asked him that he was a retired building contractor from New England, which for all it matters to this chronicle he may quite well have been. He had come to Puerto Rico ten years before, in search of a pleasant climate in which to take his well-earned ease, and had stayed ever since, which made him a relative old-timer in the current new era of the island's development. He had taken steps to make himself widely acquainted, had taken active part in many charitable enterprises, and was generally reputed to be a pillar of the community, a natural choice for civic committees, and a philanthropist of stature. Exactly how much wealth he had retired with was a matter of conjecture, but it was even less common knowledge that he had been able to increase his assets considerably while he appeared to be devoting all his time to good works.

It could only have been the fine hand of Fate that caused the Saint to be privileged to learn how this could be done on his very first encounter with Mr Elmer Quire.

Mr Quire never dreamed that Fate was stalking him when

he saw Simon Templar saunter through the Mallorquina in Caguas, where he was having lunch, and sit down at the next table. He gave the Saint a little more than a casual glance, as people usually did, dismissed him for the moment as an obvious tourist, and returned his attention to the man who sat nervously stirring a cup of coffee beside him.

"That's the trouble with you people," Mr Quire said severely. "One tries to help you, to bring you along and teach you to grow up. Everyone knows how hard I've worked for all of you. But you're like so many of the others, Gamma. I gave you a great opportunity, and you messed it up."

"I did my best, *señor*," said the man called Gamma.

He was obviously a native *borinqueño* of the country, a thin, middle-aged man with a lined face and anxious black eyes, and his dark clothes were neat but old and threadbare.

"Of course you say that," Mr Quire lectured him reproachfully. "A failure always says he did his best. Therefore the failure is not his fault. He won't admit that he failed because his best wasn't good enough, which would force him to try harder. That is why he never becomes a success."

"Is it my fault, *señor*, if my tomato seeds shoot up only a little bit and then die?"

"Certainly it is. They died because you didn't put chemicals in the water, as I've been trying to explain."

"When you tell me about this wonderful new way to grow tomatoes in water, without earth, you do not tell me I must put anything in the water."

Mr Quire became aware intuitively that he had an additional audience in the person of the bronzed tourist with the buccaneer's face who sat almost at his elbow, but the knowledge made him if possible only more righteous and long-suffering.

"If I told you once, I must have told you twenty times. How would you expect any plant to grow on nothing but water? You're enough of a farmer to know better than that. It has to have something to feed on. Like the fertilizer you put on the ground. The whole principle of growing vegetables hydroponically is that you put the fertilizer directly into the tanks of water that your plants grow in."

"You did not tell me, *señor*," Gamma said doggedly.

"I told you, but you must have forgotten. Or you just weren't paying attention. That's what I mean about how hard it is to do anything for you people. You don't concentrate. You half learn something, and go off half cocked, and then wonder why it doesn't work."

The man sipped his coffee and stirred it again glumly. Mr Quire continued to eat. There was a long silence which Mr Quire quite imperturbably allowed to run its natural course.

"If I put in chemicals now, and new seed," Gamma said at last, "will the tomatoes grow?"

"Certainly."

"Then I must do that."

"Exactly."

"But," Gamma said, "I have no money to do it."

Mr Quire seemed surprised.

"None at all?"

"*Señor*, you know that the little I had, and all that you lent me, was spent to build the tanks in which the tomatoes would grow. And from my friends I already borrow all that I can to eat."

"Then how will you go about it?" asked Mr Quire with fatherly interest.

The man licked his lips.

"I thought, *señor*, perhaps, if you would lend me a little more..."

Mr Quire's frown was almost a benediction.

"My dear man, that's quite impossible! I lent you everything I could spare to help you start this hydroponic business."

"But I will pay you as soon as the tomatoes grow—"

"But it'll be weeks, even months, before they're ready for market. Think of all the time you've wasted on that first crop that died. You should have been getting money from them already to meet your first payment to me, which is overdue right now. I'm not a rich man, Gamma. I need that money back. In fact, I must have it at once."

"I cannot pay you now, *señor*."

Mr Quire pursed his lips worriedly.

"That's really too bad," he said. "It means I shall have to take your land."

"You cannot do that!"

"Tut, tut, man. Of course I can. Or are you forgetting again? When you borrowed that money, you signed a paper giving me the right to take your land in full settlement if you were ever behind in your payments. You're behind now, and I have to get my money back somehow."

"If you do that, how shall I live?"

"You'll get a job," Mr Quire said heartily, "like anyone else. All these new factories are crying for workers, and they train you free. I'll be glad to give you a recommendation."

"But my wife, *señor*—"

"Probably I can get her a job too," Mr Quire said magnanimously. "Between you, you might easily earn more than you ever could from growing tomatoes."

'She will have a new baby very soon,' Gamma said in a dull voice. "And already there are four to take care of. . . ."

Mr Quire put a last large piece of pork chop into his mouth, and mopped his plate with a piece of bread.

"Really," he said, "sometimes I don't think I'll ever understand you people. I suppose most of you are Catholics and the rest are just irresponsible. Anyway, you breed like rabbits and then you expect special consideration because you've got too many children to support. I'm truly sorry for you, but it isn't my fault that you've got a bigger family than you can afford. You should have thought about that before you had them. Why, if I gave money away to everyone on this island who just happens to be poor, I'd be a pauper myself before dinner."

Gamma sat with his shoulders hunched, staring haggardly at the table.

Presently he said, with a sort of frightened hesitancy: "You spoke of the new factories, *señor*. My land is on the main road they are building over to Ponce. Perhaps some company would like to buy it. We could sell it for a good price, and I would pay you back and have something to start over again."

"I'll certainly have to try and sell it to somebody," said Mr

Quire. "But it isn't your land any more. It's mine, to do what I like with – or will be as soon as I record that paper you signed."

Gamma raised his eyes slowly, and they glowed with a dark pain and understanding that made them hot pools in his tense tortured face.

"*Señor,*" he said, "they speak of you as a good man, but now I think you are a devil!"

Mr Elmer Quire sat quite still, but a deep flush crept out of his collar and climbed up into the roots of his hair, mantling his rosy complexion with rich purple as it rose. His bright eyes were no longer twinkling, but became glassy and seemed to protrude. His head still kept up its slight monotonous nodding, but now the movement seemed to acquire a sinister and deliberate emphasis.

At last his voice came, a hoarse choking splutter of incredibly low-pitched violence.

"How dare you. How dare you speak to me like that. You ungrateful wretch. After all I've done for you. You made a straightforward business deal, and now because you can't keep your end of the bargain you justify yourself by insulting me. Next thing, you'll be going to some damned shyster lawyer and trying to wriggle out of the whole thing. Well let me tell you something. That paper you signed is legal, and I'll defend it all the way to the Supreme Court if I have to, if it costs me ten thousand dollars. And let me tell you something else. You go around talking like that, and I'll have you in jail. There's a law to stop you saying things like that about me, and you'd better find out about it damn quick. And if I ever hear that you've repeated a lie like that, I'll not only have the police after you, I'll see that you never get any kind of job as long as you live – or your wife, or your unwashed brats either!" The strangling voice paused and gathered itself for one last burst. "Now get out of my sight before I lose my temper!"

Gamma got to his feet, pale and shaken, but he managed to start to speak.

"It is not right, *señor*—"

"*Get out!*" said Mr Quire in a whisper of such concentrated viciousness that the man turned and stumbled hurriedly away in an almost superstitious panic.

Mr Quire wiped his brow with a snowy handkerchief.

The congestion subsided slowly from his face, and he began to unwrap a cigar.

In spite of the intensity of the paroxysm, his rage had been so muted that in the general chatter and clatter of the restaurant not a word might have been audible at a distance of more than six feet. But he remembered that the tourist with the pirate's profile at the next table was within that range, and turned to find a disconcertingly cool gaze resting steadily on him.

"Well, bless my soul," said Mr Quire with disarming joviality. "I do believe I was getting quite steamed up."

"I only thought you were going to have a stroke," said the Saint mildly, and refrained from adding that he had hoped to see it.

Mr Quire lighted his cigar.

"Some of these people would try the patience of a saint," he remarked unconsciously. "You must have heard some of the conversation, so you may have gotten a rough idea. They're like overgrown children – full of quick enthusiasms without the stamina to carry them through, hopelessly inefficient on details, and sulky when they upset their own applecarts."

"Who was your problem child?"

"Pedro Gamma. A nice fellow, but a hopeless bungler. I'm afraid I'll have to write him off as one of my failures."

"It seemed to me," Simon said with no expression, "that he might have been entitled to another chance."

"You don't know how many chances I've given him already," Mr Quire said heavily. "It's the only hobby I've got, trying to help these people. You've got to expect some disappointments. And you have to know when to take a firm line, even though it's heartbreaking sometimes." Mr Quire dismissed the subject with a final shrug of noble resignation. "You're a visitor here, I take it?"

Simon nodded.

"Sort of."

"Not in any kind of business?"

"I might get into some," said the Saint thoughtfully.

The notion had only occurred to him in the last few minutes. Mr Quire took out his wallet, extracted a card, and passed it over.

"If I can be of any help to you, give me a call. I've been here for ten years, so I know my way around pretty well. And I'm really interested in anything that's good for the island." He stood up. "Please feel free to take me up on that, any time."

Simon read the name and address, and put the card away carefully, and looked up to see Mr Quire chatting genially with the proprietor at the entrance as he paid his bill. It was obvious that he was a well-known and favoured customer. There was a parting gust of cordial amenities as he went out, and through the window Simon watched him climb into a large black Cadillac and drive away.

The Saint finished his own meal presently, and also went to the front counter with his bill.

"Do you know Mr Quire well?" he asked, in conversational Spanish.

"*Si, señor. Muy bien.*"

"What sort of man is he?"

"A very respected man, *señor*. He does much good for Puerto Rico."

"He rather likes to have things his own way, doesn't he?"

The proprietor raised his shoulders discreetly.

"If he likes someone, he will do anything in the world for him. But I should not like to cross him. He has a strong character."

"That is one way to describe him," said the Saint.

3

"IT'S A really interesting prison," said Tristan Brown, as he drove her away. "The men almost seem happy to be there. There's practically nothing to stop them escaping, as you saw; but when they do, they usually come back by themselves in a few days, and explain that they had to go to a funeral, or attend to some business, or maybe just needed a night out."

"It's probably more comfortable than home to a lot of them," said the Saint. "And most of 'em wouldn't be habitual criminals. Just nice normal guys who gave way to a natural impulse to stick a knife in somebody who got out of line."

"The warden is doing quite a job of making them over, anyway. He's a rare type – a natural philanthropist."

Simon glanced at her.

"Could he qualify for an Ogden H. Kiel endowment?"

"He might. You see, we don't just write cheques to organized charities, and yet we obviously can't deal with thousands of individual cases. So in each area we go into, we try to find a good local administrator, give him an allocation, and leave the handling of it to his judgment."

"Doesn't that get you besieged by all kinds of phonies who think what a good thing they could make for themselves out of it?"

"It would if they knew what I was doing. But you haven't read any publicity about my visit have you? Because I haven't told anyone except you. For the other people I meet, I'm just a gadabout social worker nosing around."

"And I still couldn't qualify?"

It was the perfect cue for her to begin to hint that perhaps he might qualify after all – if, for instance, he could produce a large amount of cash as evidence of his solvency and bona fides. If that was how the routine was to go. But she shook her head.

"I'm sorry. Now please stop making me think you're only interested in me because of Mr Kiel's money, and tell me what you've been up to."

"I've been studying another type who won't qualify – even more definitely."

He gave her a detailed account of his inadvertent eavesdropping on Mr Elmer Quire, and was grateful that she quickly grasped its implications, for the subtlety of Mr Quire was not easy to convey at second hand.

"The restaurant proprietor scored it right in the bull's-eye, whether he knew it or not," he said at the conclusion. "'He'll do anything in the world for you if he likes you, but don't cross him.' It sounds fine, doesn't it? A stalwart salty character. But think about it a bit longer, and you find it's the perfect description of the worst kind of spoiled selfish brat. Sweet as pie if he gets his own way, and a son of a bitch if he doesn't. The only difference is that Quire is older in years and has some power and dough to back it up. The 'little tin god' cliché was coined for him. He's an arrogant, wilful, egotistical chiseller masquerading as a big-hearted Lord Bountiful, a hypocrite so hungry for flattery and so terrified of the truth that any criticism turns him literally blue with rage. I saw it happen. Take it from me, Tristan – when you hear a man spoken about like that, look out. You're getting the lowdown on a bastard."

"If you go on like that you're going to turn blue yourself," she said, and he suddenly grinned apology.

They drove up through the dense tropical rain-jungle, stopped to pick and taste wild strawberries that were brilliantly red and totally flavourless, and went on to the lodge near the summit, where they sat and drank beer on a terrace that looked out over a whole quadrant of the island. It was one of those rare clear days on El Yunque, which is usually wreathed with dripping clouds, and towards the north they could see all the way to the coast and the deep blue of the ocean beyond. And then the daylight was fading and a chill came in the air, and they drove down again and stopped for cocktails at a place where orchids grew in the open, and stayed to eat dinner with the city lights spread out far below them. It made a day to remember.

But as they drove down again into the soft warmth of Santurce, and she was a little sleepy, and they did not have to talk so much, he was thinking again about Elmer Quire, and she knew it telepathically.

She said: "Are you going to do something about that man?"

"I might, one of these days," he said. "When I can't have this much fun with you."

"Then opportunity is just around the corner," she said. "I'm starting off early tomorrow, to go around the island, to

Mayagüez and Ponce. I'm still a working girl. I'll be gone for a couple of days."

"What's wrong with this car?"

"A local judge and his wife are taking me. And I can't get out of that, because he's a former classmate of one of my bosses. Besides, I have to maintain some reputation."

"The first reason was good enough. You didn't have to add such a dull one."

She snuggled a little closer.

"In case you think I'm a prude," she said, "I was planning to invite you to my room for a nightcap anyway."

When he came down to breakfast the next morning she had already left; but there were two cablegrams in his box.

The first one he opened verified that Tristan Brown was indeed a graduate of Columbia Law School. The second said:

GLAD CONFIRM TRISTAN BROWN OUR FULLY ACCREDITED REPRE-
SENTATIVE WILL APPRECIATE YOUR CO-OPERATION
                                        JAMES TANTRUM
                                OGDEN H. KIEL FOUNDATION

So the improbable story was true, after all, as improbable stories occasionally could be. It made him feel even better.

But it still left him with time on his hands and nothing but the matter of Mr Elmer Quire on his mind – which, for the Saint, was a highly unstable state to be in.

Mr Quire was in the small office he maintained in San Juan, in conference with a vice-president of an Alabama textile mill, when the phone call came.

"I couldn't think of a better location for your factory," he was saying. "It's right outside Gaguas, on the new four-lane highway to Ponce. Electricity, water, fine transportation, and plenty of labour to draw on. Used to be a hydroponic tomato farm, but it's nice level ground and naturally worth a lot more as an industrial site. They're good hard-working people around there, educated enough to learn fast, and yet they still aren't demanding the kind of wages you're used to paying. With the tax exemption you'll get ... Excuse me."

126

He picked up the phone.

"Yes," he said. "Yes. . . . The Mallorquina at Caguas? Yes, of course. I do remember. . . . Certainly. . . . Delighted. . . . Well, I'm going to be busy this afternoon. How about a small libation later? . . . Fine. Suppose you meet me at the Club Nâutico at six o'clock. . . . Not at all, it'll be a pleasure!"

4

To Mr Quire, the word 'pleasure' began to seem a wholly inadequate description of their meeting. After he had listened attentively for some time, he felt like a man who had been personally introduced to Santa Claus.

"Do you mean," he said, "that the Ogden H. Kiel Foundation would consider handing me, say, a million dollars to disburse here as I saw fit?"

"That would be the idea," said the Saint. "You see," he went on, glibly appropriating the speech which Tristan Brown had generously provided for him, "we don't just write cheques to organized charities, and yet we obviously can't deal with thousands of individual cases. So in each area we go into, we try to find a good local administrator, give him an allocation, and leave the handling of it to his judgment."

"There is certainly a lot of good to be done here," said Mr Quire, nodding even more rapidly. "When the sugar market collapsed, the Puerto Ricans didn't stop breeding. We've got the densest population on any American soil, more than six hundred to the square mile, and still growing. Even all the new industry that's been coming in can't absorb them. I'm afraid there will always be hardship here. But may I ask, why did you happen to think of me?"

"As soon as I started to make inquiries. I kept hearing your name mentioned as a real local philanthropist."

"I have tried to do my small best for the island since I settled here," Mr Quire said modestly. "Being retired from business, it keeps me occupied and helps me to feel I'm not altogether useless." His bright eyes blinked keenly through his glasses. "Now we come to that, by the way, I don't think I even know your name – or didn't I hear it?"

The Saint did not hesitate for an instant.

"Brown," he said. "Tristan Brown." With unsurpassable confidence he added: "I know this must seem a rather fantastic situation, but it's easy for you to check up on. Just send a wire to the Ogden H. Kiel Foundation in New York and ask them about me."

Mr Quire continued to gaze at him shrewdly.

"Then our meeting the other day wasn't entirely an accident?"

"No, it was purely coincidence. But when your name came up, I remembered having seen you in action, so to speak." The Saint frowned. "To be perfectly frank, I've been just a little worried about that."

"In what way, sir?"

"About the last things you said to that man."

"Gamma?" Mr Quire smiled. The smile ripened gradually into a resonant jolly chuckle, deep in his chest, the chortle of a good guy enjoying a good joke. "My dear fellow! How you must have misunderstood me. But of course you're new to these parts. Puerto Ricans are Latins, and they're used to violent expressions. In fact, they don't understand any other kind. And now and again you have to scold them, just like you would a child, and let them know you mean business. Certainly, I was putting the fear of God into Pedro, because that's what he needed. But by this time he's thought it over, and we'll be able to work something out. Before we're finished, he'll be telling everyone I'm his best friend."

"I'm glad to hear that." Simon looked relieved. "Because our investigation has to be very thorough. As a matter of fact, one of our requirements is to have the person we are considering submit a list of everyone he has done any kind of business with for the past five years. Then we interview all those people; and naturally, if any of them gives the impression that he's had a raw deal, or been taken advantage of in any way, the application is probably dropped right there. Would you be prepared to go along with that?"

Mr Quire rubbed his chin.

"A list like that would take me a little time," he said. "But, yes, I could let you have one."

"There's just one other thing," said the Saint.

Since he had already stolen so much of Tristan Brown's material, he saw no reason to waste the rest of the act which he had projected for her in his own sceptical mind and unjustly suspected her of leading up to.

"The late Mr Kiel," he said, "started off keeping his money in an old sock and never really got used to the idea of banks. And financial statements, to him, were just a way for clever accountants to make a bankrupt look prosperous. His will expressly forbids us to accept referees of that kind. But obviously we have to have some guarantee that the person we're considering is sufficiently well off not to be tempted by the opportunities we'd be giving him. So we ask him to show us a substantial amount of cash."

"What sort of amount, Mr Brown?"

"At least twenty thousand dollars. We have to see it in actual currency. Then it's deposited somewhere – in the applicant's own name, of course – and has to stay there until our investigation is completed. The object is just to establish that he has that kind of money that he can get along without."

Mr Quire put his fingertips together. Simon had the impression that if he had been a cat he would have purred.

"Of course I can meet that condition too. But you're giving me quite a lot to do. When would you want to go into all this?"

"The sooner the better."

Mr Quire made a rapid calculation. The Saint could visualize every step of it as if he looked into Mr Quire's mind through a window. So long to set things right with certain people like Pedro Gamma, who might expose embarrassing angles of his philanthropy. So long to get a cable reply from New York – for although Mr Quire's cupidity might rise to the right bait as quickly as anyone's, he was not the volatile type that gulps down the Colossal Lie without a test. But with the wire he had himself received from New York warm in his pocket, and the exact wording of it clear in his memory, Simon could envisage that prospect with complete equanimity.

"How about the day after tomorrow?"

"That suits me," said the Saint. "Why not meet me for lunch at my hotel?"

The hotel he named was not the one where he and Tristan were staying, but the one where he intended to register forthwith under his borrowed name.

"I'll be there at one," said Mr Quire. "And I'll try to bring my deposit."

"And I hope," said the Saint cordially, as they shook hands, "that we'll soon be entrusting you with a lot more than that."

He took one of his suitcases to the other hotel and checked in, and decided to have dinner and sleep there. The rest of the evening seemed flat and unpromising. He missed Tristan Brown, and wished she had been available for some sort of celebration that would have supplied an outlet for his suppressed exhilaration – even though he knew that her providential absence was as valuable to this stage of the story as his fortunate meeting with her had been to its early development.

He was up very early the next morning, for he had certain errands to do which included another drive to Caguas and, later, the making of airplane reservations. But those things only occupied him until lunch. He drove out for a swim at Luquillo Beach and lay on the smooth sand until sundown, and went back to his original hotel hoping that Tristan would have returned. She still hadn't come in by eight o'cock, and he went out to dinner and then to the Club 88 where he tried to divert himself with some of the amenable ladies who frequented the bar. But he couldn't develop even a superficial interest, and gave it up early and went home. Tristan was still away.

The next morning was better. The impatient excitement that the Saint always felt at the approaching climax of a beautifully dovetailed plot, as a mechanical craftsman might be enraptured by the working of an exquisitely contrived machine, was subordinated to the solid purpose of wrapping it up and handing it over to history. He slept late and luxuriously breakfasted, sunned, swam, shaved, showered, and dressed himself with detailed care and enjoyment, as if to make himself feel that everything behind him was perfect and ready for the crowning touch of perfection to come.

He took care to be waiting in his room at the right hotel for Mr Quire to announce his arrival from the lobby, and came down to the meeting like a buccaneer to the deck of a prize.

It made no difference to him that the basic routine was one of the oldest in the time-honoured confidence game. It was the rightness, the aptness, the neatness, and the justice of the situation that made it worth while; and he could no more have withheld anything from his performance than an actor with grease paint in his veins could have walked through the part of Hamlet.

"Here is the list you asked for," said Mr Quire, when they were settled in a corner of the terrace bar with a couple of tall frosted Pimm's Cups.

Simon scanned through the closely typewritten sheet and observed that the name of Pedro Gamma was on it.

"And here," said Mr Quire, "is the money."

He produced a thick bundle of hundred-dollar bills. Simon nonchalantly began to count them.

"I hope you're not worried about giving this to me," he murmured.

"Not a bit," said Mr Quire cheerfully. "To be honest, I did send a wire to New York, as you suggested, and I had a reply from your Mr Tantrum this morning. He gave you a good reference."

"Just the same," said the Saint, "I'd rather not be responsible for this much cash. Let's put it in the hotel safe before anything happens to it."

They went together to the hotel desk and asked for a deposit envelope. Mr Quire himself put the money in it and sealed it. The Saint took it for a moment to examine the flap and press it down more firmly, and turned very slightly to call the clerk back. In that infinitesimal moment the envelope passed under the open front of his jacket, and a duplicate which he had obtained beforehand and stuffed with a suitable number of rectangles of newspaper took its place and was handed to the clerk.

Mr Quire signed his name in the space provided on the envelope, and received the receipt. Then they went back to their drinks.

"It's okay for you to keep the receipt," said the Saint carelessly. "That part is only a formality anyhow. Just so long as we go to get the envelope back together and it hasn't been touched in the meantime. That way, I can truthfully say that your bond has been on deposit, and I don't have the responsibility for it."

"I quite understand," said Mr Quire. He took a healthy mouthful from his glass; and Simon was almost moved to compassion by the prodigious effort he made to appear unconcerned as he went on: "Er – would you have any idea how long it's likely to be?"

"Before you get your money back, or before we give you some of ours?"

"Well, both."

"If I don't have too much trouble locating the people on your list, I might be able to make my report in a week. As soon as that's done, I can release your deposit. The board in New York will act pretty promptly on my recommendation. Sometimes I've known them to send the first hundred thousand almost by return mail."

Even if Mr Quire took steps to keep in touch with several of the names on his list, which in his eagerness to see the investigation completed he would very likely do, it would be at least two days before he became seriously perturbed by the gradual realization that nobody he checked with had yet been interviewed, and at least twenty-four hours more before growing uneasiness and busier inquiries made him suspicious enough to risk going back for a peek in the envelope where his deposit was supposedly resting. Simon could therefore figure that he had a minimum of three days, and even longer with a little luck, in which to remove himself to other hunting-grounds and cover his back trail; and in an age of air travel that gave him the whole world to get lost in. But even so, the lunch that he had to sit through was an ordeal, for it was not only an anticlimacteric waste of time, but it also obliged him to listen for two hours to Mr Quire's nauseating hypocrisies about the good deeds he planned to do with his Foundation grant when he got it.

It felt more like two months before the Saint was gracefully able to escort Mr Quire through the lobby on his way out.

"Don't expect to see much of me for a few days," he said. "As a matter of fact, I noticed that some of the references you gave me were in Ponce and other towns, and I've a good mind to pack up and go touring. It'll give me a chance to see some of the island while I look them up. I'll probably do that first."

They strolled through the wide entrance. In the driveway outside, a girl with her back to them was saying goodbye to a couple in a car, a middle-aged man and woman. With an exchange of handwaves, the car drove off and she turned. It was Tristan Brown.

"I'll wait till I hear from you," said Mr Quire contentedly. "And thanks for the lunch."

She was hardly more than an arm's length away, and her momentary surprise at coming face to face with the Saint was changing to a quick smile. The Saint had no idea what his own expression was, but he became aware that Mr Quire was holding out a hand. He took it mechanically.

"It's been a great pleasure to meet you," said Mr Quire, with dreadful distinctness. "*Au revoir*, Mr Brown."

5

ALL AROUND the Saint tourists and business men, guests and visitors, doormen and taxi drivers, crisscrossed and prattled and honked about their sundry affairs; but Simon Templar felt as if he was marooned in a crystal sphere of utter stillness and isolation that shut out all sound and bustle as if it were taking place in another parallel dimension. He could see the name hit the girl's ears like an intangible blow, see her stop dead in her tracks with the smile fading frozenly from her face; he could feel the physical body that had once belonged to him shaking Mr Quire's hand and muttering some commonplace farewell, and feel her stare resting on him like a searchlight; and through each long-drawn second he waited for her voice to say something, anything, the inevitable words that would lead inevitably into an unpredictable morass of disaster.

But he heard nothing.

He watched Mr Quire cross over to his large black Cadillac, get in, and drive away. And still she had not spoken.

Then he had to look at her again.

She was still standing there, with a bellhop behind her patiently holding a light valise.

"Well," she said. "Mr Brown."

"Fancy meeting you," he said.

"Mr *Tristan* Brown, of course."

"Of course," said the Saint. He eyed her speculatively. "I suppose it wouldn't even be any use telling you I wasn't talking to Mr Quire about the Ogden H. Kiel Foundation."

"None at all. Why perjure yourself, on top of everything else?"

"All right, tell me the rest."

"I'm wondering how much bond he put up, to have himself considered as a possible administrator for Puerto Rico."

"Twenty thousand dollars, to be exact."

"In a sealed envelope which is now full of waste paper."

"I can see you've read stories."

"Dozens of them."

The conversation was definitely lagging.

Simon searched hazily for another approach, and suddenly it was literally thrown at him, in the person of a thin threadbare man who erupted from somewhere and practically flung himself on the Saint's neck. He hugged the Saint with both arms, slapped him on the back, grasped his hands and wrung them, and gargled incoherently for several seconds before he could get a word out.

"*Señor* Brown! *Le buscaba en todos los hoteles* – I know I will find you somewhere – I had to tell you—"

134

He went on in a torrent of yattering Spanish.

Simon listened for a while, and finally was able to subdue him. He turned to the girl.

"Excuse me," he said. "May I introduce Mr Pedro Gamma? I told you about him once, if you remember. He's just telling me that Mr Quire introduced him to the vice-president of a Stateside textile company who's looking for a factory site here, and gave Pedro his mortgage back and told him to make the deal on his own and just pay back the loan. So Pedro showed him the place today, and the guy grabbed it."

"*Si, señor.* And as you tell me something like this may happen when you come to see me, I ask him what you say it is worth, and he does not bargain at all. We make the escrow already – for fifteen thousand dollars!"

"I'm glad to hear it," said the Saint. "But I'm busy right now. Why don't you run along home and tell your wife?"

"*Si, señor!*" The little man beamed at Tristan. "I understand. *Perdone, señora.* But I had to tell . . ."

He scuttled away in radiant confusion.

Simon turned to the girl again.

"You see," he explained, "I also told Quire that he'd have to give us a list of all his business deals for some years back, and that they'd all be investigated. I figured that would send him rushing around to straighten out some of his old fast shuffles."

Then he saw that her smile had come back at last.

"We can't just stand here all afternoon," she said.

She looked around for the bellhop, but he had long ago put down her bag and gone off to gossip with the doorman. He came running back, but Simon gave him a coin and picked up the valise himself. He led her across the lobby to a secluded corner, and they sat down.

"Now if the defendant may ask a question," said the Saint, prodding the bag with his toe, "what are *you* doing here – with this?"

"The people I made that trip with just dropped me off, and I was going to check in."

"We had a nice cosy hotel. This is a gaudy and ghastly

tourist trap, where even the news stand has its own fancy prices on cigarettes and magazines. Why change?"

She gazed at him levelly.

"Maybe I thought I'd better stay away from someone I was getting to like too much."

"And now, to top it all, you find you've got to decide whether to turn him in to the cops."

"I don't know why I'm even hesitating. Except that he seems to manage to do such Saintly things on the side. It's a hell of a spot for a lawyer to be in." She rubbed a suddenly tired hand across her eyes. "I'll have to think...."

"Why don't you do that?" he suggested. "Take a shower – have a nap – get rested and freshened up, and meet me for cocktails and dinner. Let's be as sophisticated as that, anyway. Then you can decide whether I sleep in the hoosegow or—"

"But shouldn't you be, as the phrase goes, on the lam?"

"I'm in no hurry till tomorrow. Quire won't suspect anything for days; and when he does find out, there's a good sporting chance that he'll feel too foolish to squawk. The last thing a guy like that can face is looking ridiculous. I'm not gambling on it, but I've got plenty of time."

"All right," she said.

She stood up. He picked up her bag again and walked with her towards the desk.

"You've taken my name," she said. "Now what can I register as?"

"How about something nice and feminine," said the Saint, "like Isolde?"

She looked up at him, so shameless and debonair, so reckless and impudent even with the shadow of prison bars across his path and her own hand empowered to drop the gate on him, a careless corsair with nothing but laughter in his eyes; and her white teeth bit down on her lip.

"Oh, damn you," she said. "Damn you, damn you!"

— THE VIRGIN ISLANDS —

THE OLD TREASURE STORY

THE VIRGIN ISLANDS are named together as one geographical group but some of them belong to Great Britain and some to the United States. And thereby hangs this tale.

"You see the treasure is right in the middle," April Mallory told the Saint.

"How awkward of it," murmured Simon Templar.

Christopher Columbus discovered the islands east of Puerto Rico on his second voyage in 1493, but Spain did nothing about them. The British occupied Tortola in 1666, and enlarged their claim to the islands east of there. The islands of St Thomas, St Croix, and St John changed hands several times, but were held longest by the Danes, until Denmark sold them to the United States in 1917.

Now between the island of St John and the island of Tortola to the north-east of it runs a strip of water once called, rather pompously, Sir Francis Drake Channel, known to the buccaneers more picturesquely as the Virgin's Gangway, and shown on modern charts, in a dull modern way, as The Narrows. But today's comparatively dull name, like many prosaic modern things, is unarguably efficient, at least as a description; for the channel is most certainly very narrow, as such straits go, being in places less than two miles across.

"So what you might call the frontier ran somewhere through there," April Mallory explained. "But even the maps only show a dotted line which they call 'approximate'. Apparently England and America never had a fulldress meeting to decide exactly where to draw it. They got along fine anyway, the English on one island and the Americans on the other, with nothing to squabble about in between. Until now, when it's a question of whose sea bottom the treasure is on."

The Saint sipped his Dry Sack.

"That isn't in the script," he objected.

"What script?"

"The one Jack Donohue lent me."

"And who's he?"

The Saint sighed.

"Someone has to be kidding somebody," he said. "But I'll play it straight if you like."

"I wish you would."

"From the very beginning?"

"Please."

"All right. Columbus named them the Virgin Islands because there seemed to be an awful lot of them."

"That was in 1493."

"Christopher was thinking specifically of the legend of St Ursula and her eleven thousand virgins from Britain," said the Saint reprovingly, "who were massacred by the Huns somewhere around Cologne in stalwart defence of their virtue."

"What were they doing there?"

"I believe they'd been on a trip to Rome, among other things. A sort of medieval Girl Scouts' junket."

"When was this?"

"Oh, more than a thousand years before Christopher."

"I don't suppose England will ever replace them now," April said. "But you don't need to go back quite that far. Let's get more contemporary."

"Meaning around the time we picked each other up?"

"If you can't make it sound any more romantic."

It was true, however. An hour ago they had set eyes on each other for the first time, seated on adjacent stools at the bar of the Golden Galleon, a newly opened place of refreshment in the town of Charlotte Amalie, which is the town of the island of St Thomas; and it can be stipulated that all eyes were taken with what they saw. She had clear blue eyes and light red-gold hair and a face and figure that any pirate who ever trod those islands would have rather captured than any galleon; with the same clear blue eyes and bronze swashbuckler's face the Saint looked every inch as much a pirate as any man ever could have, even in such an imitation galleon as that. So that it had been very easy to strike up the conversation which just lately seemed to have gotten slightly out of hand.

"Okay," he said. "I know there's an outfit from Hollywood on location here, shooting footage for an epic entitled *Perilous Treasure*, in gorgeous Technicolour and colossal Cinemascope."

"I've heard of it."

"Jack Donohue is the director. He happens to be an old pal of mine. As a matter of fact, he wants me to double for the star in some skin-diving shots, on account of the hired hero is worried about sharks or something. That's why he let me read the script."

"How interesting."

"So if you're trying to hook me for some gag, darling, for publicity or anything else, I'm the wrong fish."

"I'm not talking about any movie script, and it's no gag," she said. "This is a real treasure."

Simon blinked. He could see now that she was completely serious.

"From pirates, yes?"

"In a way. It was a Spanish ship, the *Santa Cecilia*, loaded with gold from Mexico. Blackbeard the pirate got wind of her somehow, and he was waiting for her when she left Puerto Rico. He chased her around these islands, and overtook her in the Narrows. Either his gunners hit her in the powder magazine with an unlucky shot, or the Spanish captain decided to sink her rather than be captured. Anyway, she blew up and sank before the pirates could get their hands on any of the loot."

"You look very young to remember all this so clearly."

"One of my great-great-etcetera-grandfathers sailed with Blackbeard for a while. He kept a diary, and he drew a chart in it that shows exactly where the *Santa Cecilia* went down."

"Didn't Blackbeard or anyone else try to fish up her cargo before it got barnacles on it?"

"She sank in about eighty feet of water, and they couldn't swim down that far. They didn't have any diving apparatus in those days."

"But since then."

"The diary was handed down from father to son, and some-one was always going to do something about it, but I suppose they got a little more sceptical with each generation, and some-how nobody ever quite got around to it. Until me."

"And you spill the whole thing to the first stranger you meet in a bar," Simon remarked pensively.

She shook her head.

"I'm not quite that dumb. I heard you give your name in that last shop you were in, and I followed you."

"I didn't see you."

"I hope not. I was trying on a bathing suit in the back room. But they told me which way you'd gone. The pick-up was entirely mutual. I thought a damsel in distress could trust the Saint."

Simon nodded, and lighted a cigarette. His astonishment was already little more than a memory. An ordinary man would probably have still been gasping and goggle-eyed, if he were able to believe the girl at all; but to Simon Templar there was noth-ing too fantastic about a tale of sunken pirate treasure, or that it should be told to him. In fact, the really extraordinary thing was that in all the time he had spent among those islands of the Caribbean which history and fiction had adorned with all the trappings of the Spanish Main, he had waited so long for his first contact with such an obvious story.

"What's your trouble?" he asked.

2

THE OTHER ingredients were almost standard for that kind of situation.

April was the last direct descendant of the Mallory who had sailed with Blackbeard. Her father had been shot down in Korea. April grew up and went to business school, and after various experiments had risen to be an editorial assistant in a publish-ing house, where for forty hours a week in the office and un-counted hours at home she wrestled with strictly literary if not always literate adventure. When her mother had died not long ago, and April had found herself not only relieved of the responsibility of a partial dependent but the heiress to a nest egg of almost eight thousand dollars, she had realized that such an opportunity was never likely to knock again, and had decided to take one reckless fling at real adventure before resigning herself to the relatively humdrum alternatives of marriage or career or their combination.

"So here I am," she said, "with a couple of aqualungs, and a boat that I chartered here, and that old chart. And it's true, Saint. The wreck's exactly where it's supposed to be. I saw it!"

"What did it look like?" Simon asked casually.

"Not a bit like they'd do it in the movies. But I was ready for that. You know there'd be nothing left of a wooden hull that was sunk in these waters as long ago as that. The marine worms would have eaten it all up. And the iron rusts and gets covered with coral. I'd read all about that in books."

She could have done that; but at least she wasn't trying to sell him the description of a picturesque movie-studio wreck, as one sizeable category of inventors would have done. He could still swallow the story.

"But you were able to recognize something."

"The shapes of some guns, and cannon balls, things like that – even with coral growing on them. When you see it yourself, you'll know."

"But now," said the Saint, "there has to be a villain."

"There is."

"Name?"

"You may know it. Duncan Rawl."

Simon did know it. Duncan Rawl was a professional world traveller and self-styled adventurer who had made a very comfortable living out of his own tall tales. He had been almost everywhere and done almost everything, at least according to himself; and although there were certain spoilsports who claimed to know that his familiarity with the far places and his role in the stirring incidents which he recounted had been a lot less rich and glorious than the way he told it, their voices were practically drowned in the acclaim of the largely feminine audience which bought his books and subscribed to his profitable lecture tours.

Simon also recalled other anecdotes about Mr Rawl's inclination to believe in and enlarge upon his own publicity, which had brought him into several news stories of unquestionable authenticity and somewhat less glamorous implication, which had prompted one sharp-tongued columnist to suggest revising his name to Drunken Brawl. . . . Yes, Mr Rawl had the makings of a most acceptable heavy.

"You'd met him through your job with the publisher," he said. "So when you decided to shoot your roll on this treasure hunt, you thought he was just the guy to go to for some expert advice."

"Only I didn't realize he'd be in quite such a hurry to cut himself in. I suppose I was a bit presumptuous to think I could call on him just because I'd helped to promote a couple of his books in the line of duty. I guess I'd have seen his point if he'd asked for a cash fee, or even a percentage. But I'm sort of stuffy about being told I have to do business in bed."

"Makes it too hard to concentrate, doesn't it?" said the Saint sympathetically. "And so you parted."

"But unfortunately I'd already shown him the chart."

"And let him make a copy?"

"He didn't need to. It's not that complicated. Look."

She took a folded paper from her purse and spread it out on the bar. It was a piece of thoroughly modern tracing paper, but the outlines on it were quite clear and easy to remember, even to the location of the X that marked the most important spot.

"This is my copy," she said. "I took it from the original, and left that in a safe deposit in New York. But Great-great-etcetera-grandfather was a good sailor, or he had a very good eye. If you put this next to a modern chart, you'd almost think that's what it was made from. The only difference is that the modern chart has a dotted line through the Narrows here, for the 'approximate' boundary between British and American territory, and that line just about goes through the middle of the X. The little island up there, off the tip of Tortola, is called

Great Thatch, and it's British. And the treasure seems to be just half way between there and St John, which is ours."

Simon signed to the bartender to refill their glasses, and glanced once more at the drawing. After that he could have reproduced it himself from memory, as accurately as from a photographic plate. It would not have been an altogether amazing accomplishment, and Duncan Rawl would not have needed to be a genius to duplicate it.

"So you located the wreck," said the Saint. "And then what?"

"I'd been down with a mask and the acqualung for nearly an hour – I'd probably have been down all day if my air hadn't started to run low. When I came up, there was another launch beside my boat, and it was flying the British flag. Duncan Rawl was running it, and besides his crew he had three native police from Road Town, on Tortola. They claimed we were in British waters and we had no right to be trying to salvage anything there."

"But it was all right for Rawl to try?"

"He'd set up a British company with a couple of native stooges, and he had a licence and everything."

"So?"

"All I could do was argue that we were on the American side of the line, and try to talk everything to a standstill. I waved the Stars and Stripes and talked fast about Washington and ambassadors and the resident. Those British cops are honest fanatics about legality and protocol, even way out here, and I got them worried enough to make them decide that the only safe thing for them was to halt everything until somebody higher up settled the problem. Even Rawl couldn't persuade them to let him go ahead and dive. I figured the treasure would at least be safe for a while, and I came back here and hired a lawyer."

"When was that?"

"Just over a week ago."

The Saint relaxed.

"Oh, for a moment I thought it was urgent. Now I see your problem. A decision will be handed down in about forty years, and you're wondering how your grandchildren will make out."

"No. It might have been that way, but the American Governor and the British Governor are good friends. The British Governor comes over here to play golf, and the American Governor goes over there to fish. So they got everybody together and decided they ought to be able to settle it without any international complications. The first thing they said was, why didn't we join forces and split fifty-fifty."

"Duncan would have liked that, I suppose."

"But I wouldn't. Maybe he's got just as much legal right to anything he can find as I have, but I'm prejudiced."

"I don't blame you."

"So then they said, all right, suppose we agreed to dive on alternate days, and each kept what we brought up."

"Subject to taxes and other lawful tribute, no doubt."

"Of course. And if I hadn't agreed to that, you'd have been right, everything would have been tied up for forty years."

"When does this deal go into effect?"

"On Monday. And Duncan Rawl gets first crack!"

Simon raised his eyebrows.

"How come?"

"Those two Solomons decided that the only impartial way to settle that was to flip a coin for it. And I lost."

The blue eyes had clouded at last, and there was a gleam of raindrops in them.

"That isn't necessarily fatal," he said.

"In clear water, as shallow as that, when we know exactly where the wreck is? In one full day, they could locate and haul up everything that didn't have to be turned up with dynamite. No, they could take out everything easy in the morning and dynamite for the hard stuff in the afternoon. What'll be left on the second day won't even pay my expenses!"

Simon scowled through a meditative smoke ring. Her estimate was probably close to the truth. Assuming that there was any such treasure to be salvaged as she had described it, the first party with a free hand for a day should be able to skim all the cream off it.

"Sounds as if we'll either have to whistle up a gale for Monday," he said, "or—"

"Or you can still settle for half, April," Duncan Rawl said.

He loomed up on the other side of the girl, leaning one elbow on the bar. Neither of them had seen him come in. But the Saint knew at once who it was, even before Rawl turned to the bartender and said, "The usual," and the bartender identified him with an impersonal, "Yes, Mr Rawl."

There had been unkind critics who said that few Hollywood actors worked as hard at looking romantic as Duncan Rawl. He had the natural advantages of a broad-shouldered six-foot-four-inch frame, and a flashing smile that could light up a handsome wilful face, even if there was a certain telltale slackening of the important lines of waist and jaw. But the carefully disordered blond curls with a battered yachting cap perched on the back of them were perhaps a little too consciously photogenic, as was a shirt of sufficiently unusual cut to suggest a theatrical costume rather than a piece of haberdashery, worn unbuttoned almost to the waist as if intentionally to display an antique gold locket hung on a gold necklace thick enough to anchor a small boat. At any rate, it could never have been said that he tried self-effacingly to look like any ordinary Joe.

"I'm not greedy," Rawl said insolently. "I'll still be satisfied with an equal partnership."

"Thank you," said the girl icily. "I don't want any charity from a crook. And I'm busy, if you hadn't noticed."

"Grow up, April. There aren't any proprietary rights to a treasure. Its finders keepers. The only reason you heard about this one first, if you'll stop and think about it, is because one of your ancestors was a criminal. So what have you got to be so righteous about?"

"So long as you're happy, why don't you just go away?"

Rawl lounged more solidly against the bar, and picked up the double shot of straight whisky which the bartender had poured. He didn't look a bit like moving.

Simon slid off his stool and came around on the other side of him.

"You heard what she said," he remarked pleasantly. "Why don't you drink that somewhere else?"

Rawl straightened up and measured him with a deliberate eye. Tall and sinewy as the Saint was, Rawl was two inches taller and forty pounds heavier. It was one of those rare occasions when the Saint looked as if he should have had more discretion. Rawl grinned confidently.

"How would you like to get it right in the kisser?"

"I'd love you to try," said the Saint mildly.

Rawl raised his glass, drank it down to the last few drops, lowered it, and then jolted the dregs straight at the Saint's face.

Incredibly, the Sain't face was not there to receive them. It moved aside in an almost instantaneous blur, and the flung liquor only sprinkled a couple of drops on his shoulder as it passed through vacant space.

As another integrated process of the same general movement, Simon's left fist sank like a depth charge into Rawl's stomach just at the bottom of his dashing décolletage. Rawl grunted and leaned forward from the middle, but he was still able to launch one vicious swing at the Saint's head. Only again the head was elusive. The swing connected with nothing but air, and Rawl's own forward momentum only added a little extra verve to the encounter between his chin and the Saint's right cross. Duncan Rawl hit the bar jarringly with his back and slid against it for a couple of yards on his way down, taking a few stools with him. His eyes were glazed before he reached the floor, and he lay there very solidly, as if he liked it there and had decided to stay.

3

"PLEASE, SIR," said the bartender courteously, "would you mind leaving now? I'm sure you could handle him again, but it's bad for business. And usually he breaks bottles."

"Please," April Mallory added for herself. "I was just going to ask if you'd take me to dinner."

"I just like to oblige everyone," said the Saint.

It hadn't exactly been a brawl to rank with the most homeric bar-room brannigans in which Simon had ever participated; but it had clinched his acceptance of April's story, and assured him that he would have no sentiment to waste on Duncan Rawl. Therefore he had no regrets about it. Besides, a flurry of that kind was practically an obligatory incident at a certain stage of any good pirate-treasure story, and the Saint was rather a traditionalist about his stories. He liked to feel that all the time-honoured trimmings were in their proper place. It encouraged a kind of lighthearted certainty that virtue, which of course he represented, would be triumphant in the end.

In this case, however, the odds against the conventionally satisfying outcome looked more forbidding as he learned more about them.

He took April to dinner at Bluebeard's Castle, where he was staying, because he had decided the first time he saw it that the view from the hillside terrace of the hotel over the landlocked harbour and the town of Charlotte Amalie could only be enjoyed to the full in the right kind of company, and the Saint also liked a seasoning of romance with his stories, which was another ancient and delightful tradition that he had no desire to violate. But almost two hours later, while they were enjoying the view to the full over coffee and cigarettes and Benedictine, he had to admit that the rest of what he had learned seemed to have closed up possible loopholes rather than opened any.

"My captain's been ordered not to take me anywhere near the Narrows before Monday, and he's too scared of losing his licence to play games. Rawl's crew is under the same orders from the Governor of the British islands," she told him. "But I can't even take you over for a look."

"You wouldn't have to go along," he said. "Since you showed me the chart, I could go straight to the spot from memory. Why couldn't I hire another boat and go there tomorrow? By the same token, what's to stop Rawl doing the same – or anyone else, for that matter?"

"Because the place has been guarded ever since this hassle started. My lawyer got the American Governor to send a

Coast Guard cutter to anchor over there to protect my interests, and as soon as it got there a boatload of police from Tortola came out and tied up alongside to watch out for the British claim. The treasure couldn't be safer until the official hunting season opens at dawn on Monday."

It was then Saturday night.

"At least we've still got about thirty hours to develop an inspiration," he said finally. "Suppose we adjourn to your hotel now, where I hear they have dancing under the stars; and see if we dream up something there."

But when he finally left her that night, considerably later, they had still not dreamed up anything that was strictly related to the problem that had brought them together. Not that either of them felt that the time had been altogether wasted . . .

"Call me when you wake up in the morning," he said, "and we'll start again."

"I can't," she said. "I've promised to go to Caneel Bay for the day with my attorney and his wife, and they've been so sweet to me that I've got to do it. Besides, he's trying to come up with a last-minute inspiration too. But I'll call you as soon as I get back."

And that was another conventional obstruction, which at the moment he could have done without.

He was picking up his key at the desk of Bluebeard's Castle when a large man heaved himself out of an armchair in the lounge with a prodigious yawn.

"What sort of an hour is this to come home?" boomed Jack Donohue. "If I'd had to wait for you much longer they were going to start charging me rent."

"You're lucky I got back at all," said the Saint. "I might have been in hospital, or in jail. Weren't you worried?"

"I could have been. They told me you'd had a gorgeous redhead to dinner, and then you'd gone off with her somewhere. But I knew she'd get wise to you fairly soon, and throw you out."

They walked across to Simon's room with a pitcher of ice, and he produced a bottle of Peter Dawson to go with it.

"Well, Jackson," he said. "Besides cadging a free nightcap and insulting me, what's on your mind?"

"Are you going to do that swimming and diving for me on Monday, or not?"

"Can't you do it yourself?"

"Yes, I could do it, but it would look like hell in the picture. You've read the script. It calls for someone who looks svelte, meaning skinny and underfed, like you. And I've got to know whether I can count on you, tonight. If not, I've got to phone New York and have someone flown down tomorrow."

Simon moved his head reluctantly, left to right.

"I'm sorry, chum. I'm sort of engaged for Monday."

"Give the girl such a time tomorrow that she won't miss you till Tuesday."

"She's tied up tomorrow."

"Then to hell with her. Make her wait for you till Tuesday."

"We have a shooting schedule for Monday, too, and it's something I can't change."

"What a louse you turned out to be," Donohue said morosely. "I should have made an actor of you when I met you in Hollywood. Then you'd have been pleading with me for a chance to work, instead of spurning me for some ginger dye job. Aren't you getting a bit old to be chasing these dizzy dolls?"

The Saint grinned.

"Didn't you know, Junior? When you get to be my age, you'll really appreciate them. And they will appreciate you for your sophistication and all the money you'll have. It's a grand old formula. And talking of formulas—"

He broke off suddenly, his face transfigured in mid-speech by a beatific thought that had illuminated his brain like a revelation from heaven. For several seconds he rolled it rapturously around in his mind, assaying all its possibilities of perfection.

"Well?" Donohue said coldly.

"I'm thinking of your corny script. And I will double in those underwater shots for you."

"Thank you."

"On Tuesday."

"Monday."

"No, I'm booked even more solid on Monday now. Just switch your schedules for the two days. I'm sure you can do it."

"All right, damn you," Donohue said resignedly. "I expect you'll sink like a stone on Tuesday, but all right. If that's all it's costing me, I'll switch the schedule for you."

"It isn't *quite* all. . . ."

The director groaned aloud.

"What else? You want real mermaids to fan you between takes?"

"I don't want to strain your budget. But since you don't have to worry about getting a professional swimmer tomorrow, and you'll have nothing but time on your hands, you're going to have to do something for me."

4

THE NARROWS on Monday morning had the air of a maritime picnic ground rather than the site of a salvage operation. The US Coast Guard cutter would have been dwarfed by a destroyer, but she looked big enough to be the mother of the brood of other craft gathered around her. The police boat from Road Town and the pinnace that had brought the Governor of the British islands were tied up to one side of her, and April Mallory's chartered cabin cruiser was tied up to the other side. Duncan Rawl's launch was hove to only a few yards away.

It was a perfect day for a picnic or for salvage. The water was oily calm, silver blue and turquoise, as the sun took its first step up into a cloudless sky; and the variety of flags called for by the nations and services and personages represented gave the little group of boats a festive and holiday appearance.

"I'm only surprised that everything else in the Caribbean that'll float isn't here," said the Saint.

"All of us tried our best to keep it quiet," April said. "That was about the only thing everyone was agreed on, including the authorities. If it had got into the papers, it'd 've taken the

American and British navies combined to keep the channel clear."

The American Governor was on board the cutter, where he was playing host to the British Governor, and he had courteously invited April and the Saint aboard as soon as they came within hailing distance.

It had been nine o'clock the previous night before Simon talked to her on the phone.

"I had to have dinner with them," she said, "and now I'm full of sun and sleepy, and we've got to leave tomorrow before daylight. Don't let's try to meet tonight."

"Did your legal beagle produce his brainstorm?" he asked.

"No. Did you?"

"Yes."

She was silent for a moment.

"I'm too tired to be teased, darling."

"And I don't want to give you any false hopes, baby. It might work, but it's only a wild wild gamble. So I won't say anything now. Get some sleep, and I'll see you on the dock."

But when they had met, before dawn, and the cabin cruiser droned out through Pillsbury Sound under the paling stars, he still refused to tell her any more.

"Let's face it," he said. "You're prettier than most actresses, but you may not be one. And if you just act naturally it'll be better than any performance."

"I think I'd rather not know, anyway," she said listlessly. "I've been trying to get used to the idea that I'm licked, and it wouldn't be much fun to start hoping and be let down all over again."

Now, as they stood on the cutter's deck watching Duncan Rawl preparing for his first dive, Simon could feel that she was somewhat less stoical than she might have wished to be, and he was scarcely surprised. He was aware of more than a mild tingle of anticipation himself, although it was necessarily in a different key from hers.

Stripped down to his swimming trunks, Duncan Rawl looked like a heroic if slightly debauched and hungover Norse god. He had declined to board the cutter or to tie up to her, cutting his engine a few lengths away and letting the launch drift by to the separate focal spot befitting the star of the show. He had ignored April and the Saint in his greetings as he passed as if he had not even seen them. He sat with his feet dangling over the side, scowling down at the water, while his helpers hung the air tanks on his shoulders and put a weighted belt around his middle.

The sun was barely high enough to send light under the water when he pulled down his mask, put on the breathing mouthpiece, and let himself down till he sank out of sight.

"I suppose it'd be wicked to hope that a shark bites him," April said.

"Could be," said the Saint. "But let's hope it anyway."

He lighted a cigarette and forced himself to smoke it unhurriedly. In that way, disciplining himself against the temptation to look at his watch every few seconds, he could estimate fairly accurately that it was less than ten minutes before Rawl surfaced again, and his spirits leaped as he saw it.

Rawl's men helped him aboard and lifted off his air tank. There was a brief excited colloquy, and then one of the men took the wheel and the engine coughed and started. Rawl sprang up on to the foredeck as the launch eased over to the cutter, and as it drew alongside he was tall enough to grasp a stanchion on the cutter and hold on, mooring the launch with his own arm.

"Ahoy there, Captain, or whoever's in charge!"

The Coast Guard skipper came to the rail, but the two Governors were at his elbow, and April and the Saint were close beside them.

"What is it, Mr Rawl?"

"You'd better get these boats moved away. I'm going to dynamite."

"Already?" April gasped.

Simon cleared his throat, and moved in still closer.

"Pardon me, your Excellencies," he said to the two Governors, "but Miss Mallory asked me to come as her adviser because her attorney had to be in court this morning. And I think she has a right to protest against what Mr Rawl proposes to do."

"On what grounds?" asked the British Governor.

"To use dynamite now, before the bottom has been thoroughly examined as it is, could obliterate a lot of treasure that otherwise might be quite easy to locate and bring up – for someone who really knows what he's doing, I mean. Of course nobody would mind Mr Rawl making a mess down there if he were the only person concerned. But he should be obliged to leave Miss Mallory a fair chance to find something when her turn comes tomorrow."

"What would you suggest?" asked the American Governor.

"I think it would only be fair to let each party make a thorough search of the bottom without any blasting, before letting one party change the situation so drastically."

"I'm not dynamiting to see what it uncovers, sir," Rawl said. "I've got to do it to kill something that wouldn't let anyone do any searching."

Simon stared down at him clinically.

"You look rather pale, Duncan, old grampus," he observed. "What was it frightened you down there?"

"Only the biggest damned octopus that anyone here will ever see," snarled Rawl. "It's thirty feet across if it's an inch – and it's sitting right where the treasure is supposed to be!"

The Saint's expression was a masterpiece of derisive disbelief.

"Was it a pink one," he inquired, "wearing a green top-hat and tartan pants, and playing a duet with itself on two piccolos?"

Rawl's face turned dusky under his tan, and his muscles tensed as if to haul himself aboard the cutter by the stanchion he held.

And then a light of hellish inspiration overspread the darkness of rage and his snarl modulated into a sneer.

"Maybe you'd like to go down and see for yourself," he said.

"I'd love to," Simon said calmly. "Can we take that as an official offer – that since you're scared to go on without blowing that poor little squid to bits, you'll step aside while I try it for April?"

"You're goddam right you can," Rawl said triumphantly. "And I'm going to laugh myself sick watching the great Saint run away from that poor little squid."

April was clinging to the Saint's arm.

"I won't let you," she said.

"You will, honey," he said out of the side of his mouth. "You've got to. It's your only chance."

"Just one more thing, though," Rawl said. "If I let you in ahead of your turn, time's being wasted, and after the Saint comes back with his tail between his legs we'll have to dynamite anyway, and then it'll be hours before the water settles down again so anyone can see anything, so I should have tomorrow to myself as well."

"We'll accept that," Simon said grimly.

The two Governors stepped aside and conferred together, but not for long. The American announced their decision:

"Since our main object is to eliminate or avoid a dispute, any compromise that Miss Mallory and Mr Rawl agree upon must have our approval."

5

THE SAINT sank gently into the cool peacock depth, twisting and turning like a fancy high diver in slow motion to extract the utmost sensual delight from the feeling of three-dimensional freedom which only aqualung swimmers can experience, the nearest thing to the sensation of true flying that man has yet been able to achieve. The twin cylinders of compressed air on his back, so heavy and cumbersome on a deck, were such a negative burden under water that a belt of small lead weights was necessary to help him sink. Thus counterbalanced, his body felt almost weightless, so that he could turn in any direction or rest relaxed in any position without effort; or if he wished to move anywhere he only had to make lazy movements with his legs, and the rubber flippers on his feet would propel him as smoothly as the fins of a fish. Breath came to him through the mouthpiece gripped in his teeth, as much and as often as he wanted, so that there was none of the strain and struggle inseparable from ordinary swimming, no irksome reminder that he was in a foreign element. It was a strange rapture which he would discover anew every time he did it: to feel literally almost as much at home in the water as a fish, yet with a buoyant exultation more like the ecstasy of flight that a poet would attribute to a bird.

And like a bird he soared and glided through water almost as crystal clear as air, but more clinging and resistant so that all movements were more languorous, over the hills and valleys, the fantastic groves and gardens of a strange silent world. Coveys of striped and tinted small fry scattered and circled as he planed through them, and among the submarine trees larger fish moved more sluggishly; and down in the bluer deeps, sprawling torpid and obscene, was the ultimate monster – the finest plastic octopus, Jack Donohue had assured him, that any Hollywood prop department had yet constructed.

The independently traditional octopus that had a part in every self-respecting story of sunken treasure since fiction discovered diving.

It was the first time Simon had seen it properly, even though he had helped to place it in its present location. He and Donohue and the prop man had been out there the day before on the tugboat which Donohue was using for his water work, ostensibly to scout scenery and make preparations for the following week's shooting: the tugboat and Donohue were already known to the Coast Guard crew, and were allowed to approach without being warned off as brusquely as any other boat would have been. Simon and the prop man had dumped the deflated monster over the far side of the tug two hundred yards away and dragged it into position under water, while Donohue took the tug alongside the cutter and engaged the crew in conversation; and the keels of the two boats, which they could look up and see, provided a perfect marker for the position that Simon had to find. But then Simon had had trouble with his air regulator valve, and had had to jettison his weights and swim upwards hastily, leaving the prop man to complete the installation and inflation alone. He had steered his rise to the side of the tug away from the Coast Guard cutter, and climbed aboard where the tug's deckhouse hid him, and soon afterwards the prop man had done the same, and then Donohue had promptly headed the tug away down the channel before they would seem to be dawdling too long in the forbidden area.

It had all worked out as slickly as a drill; and even the prop man had only been told that Donohue was determined to shoot some underwater scenes in that particular spot in spite of the prohibition.

Now that Simon saw the monster (which in their irreverent way the movie unit had christened Marilyn) in its full glory, he was ready to agree that it was a real work of art. Some of its tentacles which were not anchored to the rock, stirred no doubt by unseen tidal currents, moved sinuously like huge slothful snakes, and their undulating motion transmitted an effect of ponderously pulsing life to the bloated purple body and the malignant liquid eyes. He couldn't despise Rawl for being scared. If he hadn't known what it was, he wouldn't have gone anywhere near it himself.

But it had worked, psychologically and with shrewd needling, exactly as the Saint had banked on it.

Now all he had to do was pick up the gold and load it into the cradle which had been lowered from April's cruiser.

It seemed almost absurdly anticlimatic, but that was about all there was to it.

It was the kind of sunken treasure that salvage men dream about. The *Santa Cecilia* had gone down in a rocky basin which kept her remains together as if in a bowl. There were no shifting sands, the bane of most treasure hunts, to scatter and swallow them. Everything that had not perished was within a small radius; and he had located the area without too much trouble, as April had said he would, by the suggested shapes of such recognizables as cannon and cannon balls. It was only a matter of chipping the crusts of coral at every likely-looking spot, working with hammer and crowbar whenever he was rewarded with a yellow gleam, breaking the gold bars loose and dragging them to the cradle and putting them in . . .

In only half an hour he had collected as big a load as he figured the light tackle on the cruiser could comfortably handle.

He signalled on the rope for it to be hauled up, and paddled off to investigate another promising coral formation still closer to the shelf on which Marilyn sat eyeing him balefully. Under the concealing growth of living stone, he found another mound of ingots.

He wished he could have been on the cruiser's deck, as well as down there, to share April's excitement when she saw the first load.

He started to smile, almost getting himself a mouthful of water. The excitement on the surface would not be confined to April's cruiser. It would spread in a flash to every other boat in the group – including Rawl's. Somewhat belatedly, he wondered what would happen after that.

He had told April the truth about Marilyn, of course, before he started down, in a brief moment when he had her alone. But he hadn't had time to emphasize that the secret must always be kept between them. He hoped that in her intoxication with the last-minute victory she wouldn't let something out that would reach the ears of Rawl. It would be ironic to have victory snatched from them again on a technicality. But if Rawl cried foul, the Governors might have to sustain him. Or would Rawl prefer to accept defeat rather than ridicule?

Simon had a partial answer about April in a few minutes. She came down in the empty cradle, wearing her own acqualung, like a modern mermaid in a hammock. She could not smile, with the rubber mouthpiece deforming her lips, but as he touched her and they shook hands he saw her eyes shining and dancing behind the glass of her face mask.

Then she saw the octopus, and her eyes grew still bigger. Simon got her attention back by shaking her shoulders; then as she looked at him he pointed at the octopus, then up towards the surface, then put an upraised forefinger in front of his mouthpiece. She nodded vigorously, and repeated the forefinger gesture, and he figured that everything was still all right.

But he looked up again, and saw Duncan Rawl coming down.

There was no mistaking the glint of sunlight on his yellow curls: Or the glint of metal from the powerful spear gun crouched under his arm like a lance.

The Saint's thoughts raced in a vertiginous cascade. Had Rawl gone completely crazy with disappointment, berserk, decided to murder one or both of them regardless of the almost inevitable consequences? It seemed incredible to the Saint even as he instinctively thrust April behind him and poised himself for the flimsy chance of parrying the spear with his crowbar. Rawl was swimming down at a steep angle towards them, but on a course which began to look as if it would take him down on to Marilyn unless he pulled out of the dive at the last moment. Then he was playing for some kind of compensating glory? Since the Saint had made him look foolish by ignoring the octopus and having no trouble, was Rawl thinking of vindicating himself by killing it and then claiming to have saved the Saint's life? That was plausible, yet it seemed hardly enough. A boast like that hardly seemed enough to salve a hypertrophied ego that had taken such punctures as he had administered to Rawl's.

And then the answer dawned on him, with the clarity of a blueprint, as Rawl slowed his glide directly over the giant cephalopod. It was written like a book in the way Rawl glanced towards him for an instant, running his eye like a tape measure over the distance between Simon and the octopus.

Rawl only expected his shaft when he fired it to infuriate the creature. Then it would grab Simon and April who were well within its reach. And Duncan Rawl would take credit for having valiantly tried to save them. . . .

The Saint's ribs ached from the impossibility of laughing.

Duncan Rawl fired his spear.

It twinkled like a silver arrow, straight down at Marilyn's great amorphous body. And then the thing happened that curdled and froze the laughter in Simon's chest.

As if the monster had watched everything with its basilisk eye, and hadn't been fooled for a second, knowing exactly where the thing that stung it had come from – *but how preposterous and fantastic could anything be?* – it released the rock it sprawled on and shot straight upwards like an outlandish rocket. Its tentacles lashed around Rawl like enormous whips, and where they touched they clung. He looked like a pygmy in its stupendous eight-armed grip. One of the arms coiled around his head, then writhed away again, taking with it his mask and breathing hose. The Saint and April had one last dreadful glimpse of his face, before the final horror was blotted out in a tremendous cloud of ink.

6

"IT'S A GOOD thing I only want you to do some swimming, and not as a technical expert," Jack Donohue said caustically, "if you can't tell a real octopus from a prop."

"I thought it looked extraordinarily lifelike," said the Saint. "But I've heard they can do anything in Hollywood. I should be more careful what publicity I read."

They sat out on the terrace of Bluebeard's Castle again, watching the lights kindle below them as the brief twilight deepened over the town. April was with them, but she was not talking much.

"You're lucky I don't have to send you a bill that'd keep you broke for three years," Donohue said. "Some fishermen found Marilyn drifting around Cruz Bay. She wasn't damaged much. But I'm going to be more careful the next time anyone comes to me to borrow an artificial octopus."

"The only way I can figure it, the real one must have had an unsatisfactory tussle with her," Simon said, "whether he saw her as an unwilling sweetheart or a rival male. Anyway, before he found out she was only a prop, he'd torn her loose from her moorings, and she floated away. The real octopus liked the look of the spot and decided to settle down there himself."

"And why he didn't grab you for breakfast as soon as you came within reach, I'll never know."

"Maybe he'd just had a good breakfast and wasn't hungry.

Didn't you ever go fishing and wonder why sometimes they'll bite anything and other times they seem to be on a hunger strike? Of course when Rawl shot a spear into it, that was different. Even an octopus must have its pride."

"And it was a break for you that it was smart enough to know who shot at it."

"It's too bad your camera crew wasn't there. It was a better scene than you'll ever direct."

April shuddered.

"Please don't," she said. "I know he meant it to kill us, but I'll have nightmares every time I remember that thing wooshing up at him, I never knew they could move so fast, and his face..."

"Don't let that Saint name fool you," Donohue said. "He's a ghoul. No, I take that back. He's a thing ghouls won't speak to."

"He is not!" she said indignantly. "As soon as he'd got me up to the boat, he went back to see if he couldn't do anything, even though all he had was a knife. But he couldn't see anything."

"All right," Donohue said. "He's a hero. But don't forget to count those gold bars every time he goes near them."

"He can have anything he wants," April said.

Jack Donohue finished his Peter Dawson and stood up.

"I'm expecting a call from the studio, and I've got to work on the script tonight," he said. "But before I ruin your evening by leaving you, would someone tell me why the Saint always ends up with a billion dollars and the most beautiful girl in sight?"

"Doesn't that go with every old treasure story?" said the Saint.

— HAITI —

THE QUESTING TYCOON

IT WAS intolerably hot in Port-au-Prince; for the capital city of Haiti lies at the back of a bay, a gullet twenty miles deep beyond which the opening jaws of land extend a hundred and twenty miles still farther to the west and north-west, walled in by steep high hills, and thus perfectly sheltered from every normal shift of the trade winds which temper the climate of most parts of the Antilles. The geography which made it one of the finest natural harbours in the Caribbean had doubtless appealed strongly to the French buccaneers who founded the original settlement; but three centuries later, with the wings of Pan American Airways to replace the sails of a frigate, a no less authentic pirate could be excused for being more interested in escaping from the sweltering heat pocket than in dallying to admire the anchorage.

As soon as Simon Templar had completed his errands in the town, he climbed into the jeep he had borrowed and headed back up into the hills.

Knowing what to expect of Port-au-Prince at that time of year, he had passed up the ambitious new hotels of the capital in favour of the natural air-conditioning of the Châtelet des Fleurs, an unpretentious but comfortable inn operated by an American whom he had met on a previous visit, only about fifteen miles out of the city but five thousand feet above the sea-level heat. He could feel it getting cooler as the road climbed, and in a surprisingly short time it was like being in another latitude. But the scenery did not seem to become any milder to correspond with the relief of temperature: the same brazen sun-bathed rugged brownish slopes with few trees to soften their parched contours. Most of the houses he passed, whether a peasant's one-room cottage or an occasional expensive château, were built of irregular blocks of the same native stone, so that they had an air of being literally carved out of the landscape; but sometimes in a sudden valley or clinging to a distant hillside there would be a palm-thatched cabin of rough raw timbers that looked as if it had been transplanted straight from Africa. And indisputably transplanted from Africa were the straggling files of ebony people, most of them women, a few plutocrats adding their own weight to the already fantastic burdens of incredibly powerful little donkeys, but the majority laden fabulously themselves with great baskets balanced on their heads, who bustled cheerfully along the rough shoulders of the road.

He came to the little town of Pétionville, drove past the pleasant grass-lawned square dominated by the very French-looking white church, and headed on up the corkscrew highway towards Kenscoff. And six kilometres further on he met Sibao.

As he rounded one of the innumerable curves he saw a little crowd collected, much as some fascinating obstruction would create a knot in a busy string of ants. Unlike other groups that he had passed before where a few individuals from one of the antlines would fall out by the wayside to rest and gossip, this cluster had a focal point and an air of gravity and concern that made him think first of an automobile accident, although there was no car or truck in sight. He slowed up automatically, trying to see what it was all about as he went by, like almost any normal traveller; but when he glimpsed the unmistakable bright colour of fresh blood he pulled over and stopped, which perhaps few drivers on that road would have troubled to do.

The chocolate-skinned young woman whom the others were gathered around had a six-inch gash in the calf of one leg. From the gestures and pantomime of her companions rather than the few basic French word-sounds which his ear could pick out of their excited jabber of Creole, he concluded that a loose stone had rolled under her foot as she walked, taking it from under her and causing her to slip sideways down off the shoulder, where another sharp pointed stone happened to stick out at exactly the right place and angle to slash her like a crude dagger. The mechanics of the accident were not really important, but it was an ugly wound, and the primitive first-aid efforts of the spectators had not been able to staunch the bleeding.

Simon saw from the tint of the blood that no artery had been cut. He made a pressure bandage with his handkerchief and two strips ripped from the tail of his shirt; but it was obvious that a few stitches would be necessary for a proper repair. He picked the girl up and carried her to the jeep.

"Nous allons chercher un médecin," he said; and he must have been understood, for there was no protest over the abduction as he turned the jeep around and headed back towards Pétionville.

The doctor whom he located was learning English and was anxious to practise it. He contrived to keep Simon around while he cleaned and sewed up and dressed the cut, and then conveniently mentioned his fee. Simon paid it, although the young woman tried to protest, and helped her back into the jeep.

His good-Samaritan gesture seemed to have become slightly harder to break off than it had been to get into; but with nothing but time on his hands he was cheerfully resigned to letting it work itself out.

"Where were you going?" he asked in French, and she pointed up the road.

"Là-haut."

The reply was given with a curious dignity, but without presumption. He was not sure at what point he had begun to feel that she was not quite an ordinary peasant girl. She wore the same faded and formless kind of cotton dress, perhaps cleaner than some, but not cleaner than all the others, for it was not uncommon for them to be spotless. Her figure was slimmer and shapelier than most, and her features had a patrician mould that reminded him of ancient Egyptian carvings. They had remained masklike and detached throughout the ministrations of the doctor, although Simon knew that some of it must have hurt like hell.

He drove up again to the place where he had found her. Two other older women were sitting there, and they greeted her as the jeep stopped. She smiled and answered, proudly, displaying the new white bandage on her leg. She started to get out.

He saw that there were three baskets by the roadside where the two women had waited. He stopped her, and said: "You should not walk far today, especially with a load. I can take you all the way."

"*Vous êtes très gentil.*"

She spoke French very stiffly and shyly and correctly, like a child remembering lessons. Then she spoke fluently to the other women in Creole, and they hoisted the third basket between them and put it in the back of the jeep. Her shoes were still on top of its miscellany of fruits and vegetables, according to the custom of the country, which regards shoes as too valuable to be worn out with mere tramping from place to place, especially over rough rocky paths.

Simon drove all the way to the Châtelet des Fleurs, where the road seems to end, but she pointed ahead and said: "*Plus loin.*"

He drove on around the inn. Not very far beyond it the pavement ended, but a navigable trail meandered on still further and higher towards the background peaks. He expected it to become impassable at every turn, but it teased him on for several minutes and still hadn't petered out when a house suddenly came in sight, built out of rock and perched like a fragment of a medieval castle on a promontory a little above them. A rutted driveway branched off and slanted up to it, and the young woman pointed again.

"*La maison-là.*"

It was not a mansion in size, but on the other hand it was certainly no native peasant's cottage.

"*Merci beaucoup,*" she said in her stilted schoolgirl French, as the jeep stopped in front of it.

"*De rien,*" he murmured amiably, and went around to lift out the heavy basket.

A man came out on to the verandah, and she spoke rapidly in Creole, obviously explaining about her accident and how she came to be chauffeured to the door. As Simon looked up, the man came down to meet him, holding out his hand.

"Please don't bother with that," he said. "I've got a handy man who'll take care of it. You've done enough for Sibao already. Won't you come in and have a drink? My name's Theron Netlord."

Simon Templar could not help looking a little surprised. For Mr Netlord was not only a white man, but he was unmistakably an American; and Simon had some vague recollection of his name.

2

IT CAN be assumed that the birth of the girl who was later to be called Sibao took place under the very best auspices, for her father was the *houngan* of an *houmfort* in a valley that could be seen from the house where Simon had taken her, which in terms of a more familiar religion than voodoo would be the equivalent of the vicar of a parish church; and her mother was not only a *mambo* in her own right, but also an occasional communicant of the church in Pétionville. But after the elaborate precautionary rituals with which her birth was surrounded, the child grew up just like any of the other naked children of the hills, until she was nearly seven.

At that time, she woke up one morning and said: "Mama, I saw Uncle Zande trying to fly, but he dived into the ground."

Her mother thought nothing of this until the evening, when word came that Uncle Zande, who was laying tile on the roof of a building in Léogane, had stumbled off it and broken his neck. After that much attention was paid to her dreams, but the things that they prophesied were not always so easy to interpret until after they happened.

Two years later her grandfather fell sick with a burning fever, and his children and grandchildren gathered around to see him die. But the young girl went to him and caressed his forehead, and at that moment the sweating and shivering stopped, and the fever left him and he began to mend. After that there were others who asked for her touch, and many of them affirmed that they experienced extraordinary relief.

At least it was evident that she was entitled to admission to the *houmfort* without further probation. One night, with a red bandanna on her head and gay handkerchiefs knotted around her neck and arms, with a bouquet in one hand and a crucifix in the other, she sat in a chair between her four sponsors, and watched the *hounsiscanzo*, the student priests, dance before her. Then her father took her by the hand to the President of the congregation, and she recited her first voodoo oath:

"*Je jure, je jure*, I swear to respect the powers of the *mystères de Guinée*, to respect the powers of the *houngan*, of the President of the Society, and the powers of all those on whom these powers are conferred."

And after she had made all her salutations and prostrations, and had herself been raised shoulder high and applauded, they withdrew and left her before the altar to receive whatever revelation the spirits might vouchsafe to her.

At thirteen she was a young woman, long-legged and comely, with a proud yet supple walk and prematurely steady eyes that gazed so gravely at those whom she noticed that they seemed never to rest on a person's face, but to look through into the thoughts behind it. She went faithfully to school and learned what she was told to, including a smattering of the absurdly involved and illogical version of her native tongue which they called 'French'; but when her father stated that her energy could be better devoted to helping to feed the family, she ended her formal education without complaint.

There were three young men who watched her one evening as she picked pigeon peas among the bushes that her father had planted, and who were more impressed by the grace of her body than by any tales they may have heard of her supernatural gifts. As the brief mountain twilight darkened they came to seize her; but she knew what was in their minds, and ran. As the one penitent survivor told it, a cloud suddenly swallowed her: they blundered after her in the fog, following the sounds of her flight: then they saw her shadow almost within reach, and leapt to the capture, but the ground vanished from under their feet. The bodies of two of them were found at the foot of the precipice; and the third lived, though with a broken back, only because a tree caught him on the way down.

Her father knew then that she was more than qualified to

become an *hounsis-canzo,* and she told him that she was ready. He took her to the *houmfort* and set in motion the elaborate seven-day ritual of purification and initiation, instructing her in all the mysteries himself. For her loa, or personal patron deity, she had chosen Erzulie; and in the baptismal ceremony of the fifth day she received the name of Sibao, the mystic mountain ridge where Erzulie mates with the Supreme Gods, the legendary place of eternal love and fertility. And when the *houngan* made the invocation, the goddess showed her favour by possessing Sibao, who uttered prophecies and admonitions in a language that only *houngans* can interpret, and with the hands and mouth of Sibao accepted and ate of the sacrificial white pigeons and white rice; and the *houngan* was filled with pride as he chanted:

> *"Les Saints mandés mangés. Genoux-terre!*
> *Parce que gnou loa govi pas capab mangé,*
> *Ou gaingnin pour mangé pour li!"*

Thereafter she hoed the patches of vegetables that her father cultivated as before, and helped to grate manoic, and carried water from the spring, and went back and forth to market, like all the other young women; but the tale of her powers grew slowly and surely, and it would have been a reckless man who dared to molest her.

Then Theron Netlord came to Kenscoff, and presently heard of her through the inquiries that he made. He sent word that he would like her to work in his house; and because he offered wages that would much more than pay for a substitute to do her work at home, she accepted. She was then seventeen.

"A rather remarkable girl," said Netlord, who had told Simon some of these things. "Believe me, to some of the people around here, she's almost like a living saint."

Simon just managed not to blink at the word.

"Won't that accident this afternoon shake her pedestal a bit?" he asked.

"Does a bishop lose face if he trips over something and breaks a leg?" Netlord retorted. "Besides *you* happened. Just when she needed help, you drove by, picked her up, took her to the doctor, and then brought her here. What would you say were the odds against her being so lucky? And then tell me why it doesn't still look as if *something* was taking special care of her!"

He was a big, thick-shouldered man who looked as forceful as the way he talked. He had iron-grey hair and metallic grey eyes, a blunt nose, a square thrusting jaw, and the kind of lips that even look muscular. You had an inevitable impression of him at the first glance; and without hesitation you would have guessed him to be a man who had reached the top ranks of some competitive business, and who had bulled his way up there with ruthless disregard for whatever obstructions might have to be trodden down or jostled aside. And trite as the physiognomy must seem, in this instance you would have been absolutely right.

Theron Netlord had made a fortune from the manufacture of bargain-priced lingerie.

The incongruity of this will only amuse those who know little about the clothing industry. It would be natural for the uninitiated to think of the trade in fragile feminine frotheries as being carried on by fragile, feminine, and frothy types; but in fact, at the wholesale manufacturing level, it is as tough and cut-throat a business as any legitimate operation in the modern world. And even in a business which has always been somewhat notorious for a lack of tenderness towards its employees, Mr Netlord had been a perennial source of ammunition for socialistic agitators. His long-standing vendetta against organized labour was an epic of its kind; and he had been named in one Congressional investigation as the man who, with a combination of gangster tactics and an ice-pick eye for loopholes in union contracts and government regulations, had come closest in the last decade to running an old-fashioned sweatshop. It was from casually remembered references to such things in the newspapers that Simon had identified the name.

"Do you live here permanently?" Simon asked in a conversational way.

"I've been here for a while, and I'm staying a while," Netlord answered equivocally. "I like the rum. How do you like it?"

"It's strictly ambrosial."

"You can get fine rum in the States, like that Lemon Hart from Jamaica, but you have to come here to drink Barbancourt. They don't make enough to export."

"I can think of worse reasons for coming here. But I might want something more to hold me indefinitely."

Netlord chuckled.

"Of course you would. I was kidding. So do I. I'll never retire. I *like* being in business. It's my sport, my hobby, and my recreation. I've spent more than a year all around the Caribbean, having what everyone would say was a nice long vacation. Nuts. My mind hasn't been off business for a single day."

"They tell me there's a great future in the area."

"And I'm looking for the future. There's none left in America. At the bottom, you've got your employees demanding more wages and pension funds for less work every year. At the top you've got a damned paternalistic Government taxing your profits to the bone to pay for all its utopian projects at home and abroad. The man who's trying to literally mind his own business is in the middle, in a squeeze that wrings all the incentive out of him. I'm sick of bucking that set-up."

"What's wrong with Puerto Rico? You can get a tax exemption there if you bring in an employing industry."

"Sure. But the Puerto Ricans are getting spoiled, and the cost of labour is shooting up. In a few more years they'll have it as expensive and as organized as it is back home."

"So you're investigating Haiti because the labour is cheaper?"

"It's still so cheap that you could starve to death trying to sell machinery. Go visit one of the factories where they're making wooden salad bowls, for instance. The only power tool they use is a lathe. And where does the power come from? From a man who spends the whole day cranking a big wheel. Why? Because all he costs is one dollar a day – and that's cheaper than you can operate a motor, let alone amortizing the initial cost of it!"

"Then what's the catch?"

"This being a foreign country: your product hits a tariff wall when you try to import it into the States, and the duty will knock you silly."

"Things are tough all over," Simon remarked sympathetically.

The other's sinewy lips flexed in a tight grin.

"Any problem is tough till you lick it. Coming here showed me how to lick this one – but you'd never guess how!"

"I give up."

"I'm sorry, I'm not telling. May I fix your drink?"

Simon glanced at his watch and shook his head.

"Thanks, but I should be on my way." He put down his glass and stood up. "I'm glad I needn't worry about you getting ulcers, though."

Netford laughed comfortably, and walked with him out on to the front veranda.

"I hope getting Sibao back here didn't bring you too far out of your way."

"No, I'm staying just a little below you, at the Châtelet des Fleurs."

"Then we'll probably run into each other." Netford put out his hand. "It was nice talking to you, Mr—"

"Templar. Simon Templar."

The big man's powerful grip held on to Simon's.

"You're not – by any chance – that fellow they call the Saint?"

"Yes." The Saint smiled. "But I'm just a tourist."

He disengaged himself pleasantly; but as he went down the steps he could feel Netlord's eyes on his back, and remembered that for one instant he had seen in them the kind of fear from which murder is born.

3

IN TELLING so many stories of Simon Templar, the chronicler runs a risk of becoming unduly preoccupied with the reactions of various characters to the discovery that they have met the Saint, and it may fairly be observed that there is a definite limit to the possible variety of these responses. One of the most obvious of them was the shock to a guilty conscience which could open a momentary crack in an otherwise impenetrable mask. Yet in this case it was of vital importance.

If Theron Netlord had not betrayed himself for that fleeting second, and the Saint had not been sharply aware of it, Simon might have quickly dismissed the pantie potentate from his mind; and then there might have been no story to tell at all.

Instead of which, Simon only waited to make more inquiries about Mr Netlord until he was able to corner his host, Atherton Lees, alone in the bar that night.

He had an easy gambit by casually relating the incident of Sibao.

"Theron Netlord? Oh, yes, I know him," Lee said. "He stayed here for a while before he rented that house up the hill. He still drops in sometimes for a drink and a yarn."

"One of the original rugged individualists, isn't he?" Simon remarked.

"Did he give you his big tirade about wages and taxes?"

"I got the synopsis, anyway."

"Yes, he's a personality all right. At least he doesn't make any bones about where he stands. What beats me is how a fellow of that type could get all wrapped up in voodoo."

Simon did not actually choke and splutter over his drink because he was not given to such demonstration, but he felt as close to it as he was ever likely to.

"He what?"

"Didn't he get on to that subject? I guess you didn't stay very long."

"Only for one drink."

"He's really sold on it. That's how he originally came up here. He'd seen the voodoo dances they put on in the tourist spots down in Port-au-Prince, but he knew they were just a nightclub show. He was looking for the McCoy. Well, we sent the word around, as we do sometimes for guests who're interested, and a bunch from around here came up and put on a show in the patio. They don't do any of the real sacred ceremonies, of course, but they're a lot more authentic than the professionals in town. Netlord lapped it up; but it was just an appetizer to him. He wanted to get right into the fraternity and find out what it was all about."

"What for?"

"He said he was thinking of writing a book about it. But half the time he talks as if he really believed in it. He says that the trouble with Western civilization is that it's too practical – it's never had enough time to develop its spiritual potential."

"Are you pulling my leg or is he pulling yours?"

"I'm not kidding. He rented that house, anyway, and set out to get himself accepted by the natives. He took lessons in Creole so that he could talk to them, and he speaks it a hell of a lot better than I do – and I've lived here a hell of a long time. He hired that girl Sibao just because she's the daughter of the local *houngan*, and she's been instructing him and sponsoring him for the *houmfort*. It's all very serious and legitimate. He told me some time ago that he'd been initiated as a junior member, or whatever they call it, but he's planning to take the full course and become a graduate witchdoctor."

"Can he do that? I mean, can a white man qualify?"

"Haitans are very broadminded," Atherton Lee said gently. "There's no colour bar here."

Simon broodingly chain-lighted another cigarette.

"He must be dreaming up something new and frightful for the underwear market," he murmured.

"Maybe he's planning to top those perfumes that are supposed to contain mysterious smells that drive the male sniffer mad with desire. Next season he'll come out with a negligee with a genuine voodoo spell woven in, guaranteed to give the matron of a girls' reformatory more sex appeal than Cleopatra."

But the strange combination of fear and menace that he had caught in Theron Netlord's eyes came back to him with added vividness, and he knew that a puzzle confronted him that could not be dismissed with any amusing flippancy. There had to be a true answer, and it had to be of unimaginable ugliness: therefore he had to find it, or he would be haunted for ever after by the thought of the evil he might have prevented.

To find the answer, however, was much easier to resolve than to do. He wrestled with it for half the night, pacing up and down his room; but when he finally gave up and lay down to sleep, he had to admit that his brain had only carried him around in as many circles as his feet, and gotten him just as close to nowhere.

In the morning, as he was about to leave his room, something white on the floor caught his eye. It was an envelope that had been slipped under the door. He picked it up. It was sealed, but there was no writing on it. It was stiff to his touch, as if it contained some kind of card, but it was curiously heavy.

He opened it. Folded in a sheet of paper was a piece of thin bright metal about three inches by two, which looked as if it might have been cut from an ordinary tin can, flattened out and with the edges turned under so that they would not be sharp. On it had been hammered an intricate symmetrical design.

Basically, a heart. The inside of the heart filled with a precise network of vertical and horizontal lines, with a single dot in the centre of each little square that they formed. The outline of the heart was trimmed with a regularly scalloped edge, like a doily, with a similar dot in each of the scallops. Impaled on a mast rising from the upper V of the heart, was a crest like an ornate letter M, with a star above and below it. Two curlicues like skeletal wings swooping out, one from each shoulder of the heart, and two smaller curlicues tufting from the bottom point of the heart, on either side of another sort of vertical mast projecting down from the point and ending in another star – like an infinitely stylized and painstaking doodle.

On the paper that wrapped it was written, in a careful childish script:

> *Pour vous protéger.*
> *Merci.*
>
> *Sibao*

Simon went on down to the dining-room and found Atherton Lee having breakfast.

"This isn't Valentine's Day in Haiti, is it?" asked the Saint.

Lee shook his head.

"Or anywhere else that I know of. That's sometime in February."

"Well, anyhow, I got a valentine."

Simon showed him the rectangle of embossed metal.

"It's native work," Lee said. "But what is it?"

"That's what I thought you could tell me."

"I never saw anything quite like it."

The waiter was bringing Simon a glass of orange juice. He stood frozen in the act of putting it down, his eyes fixed on the piece of tin and widening slowly. The glass rattled on the service plate as he held it.

Lee glanced up at him.

"Do you know what it is?"

"*Vêver,*" the man said.

He put the orange juice down and stepped back, still staring.

Simon did not know the word. He looked inquiringly at his host, who shrugged helplessly and handed the token back.

"What's that?"

"*Vêver,*" said the waiter. "Of Maîtresse Erzulie."

"Erzulie is the top voodoo goddess," Lee explained. "I guess that's her symbol, or some sort of charm."

"If you get good way, very good," said the waiter obscurely. "If you no should have, very bad."

"I believe I dig you, Alphonse," said the Saint. "And you don't have to worry about me. I got it the good way." He showed Lee the paper that had enclosed it. "It was slid under my door sometime this morning. I guess coming from her makes it pretty special."

"Congratulations," Lee said. "I'm glad you're officially protected. Is there anything you particularly need to be protected from?"

Simon dropped the little plaque into the breast pocket of his shirt.

"First off, I'd like to be protected from the heat of Port-au-Prince. I'm afraid I've got to go back down there. May I borrow the jeep again?"

"Of course. But we can send down for almost anything you want."

"I hardly think they'd let you bring back the Public Library," said the Saint. "I'm going to wade through everything they've got on the subject of voodoo. No, I'm not going to take it up like Netlord. But I'm just crazy enough myself to lie awake wondering what's in it for him."

He found plenty of material to study – so much, in fact, that instead of being frustrated by a paucity of information he was almost discouraged by its abundance. He had assumed, like any average man, that voodoo was a primitive cult that would have a correspondingly simple theology and ritual: he soon discovered that it was astonishingly complex and formalized. Obviously he wasn't going to master it all in one short day's study. However, that wasn't necessarily the objective. He didn't have to write a thesis on it, or even pass an examination. He was only looking for something, anything, that would give him a clue to what Theron Netlord was seeking.

He browsed through books until one o'clock, went out to lunch, and returned to read some more. The trouble was that he didn't know what he was looking for. All he could do was expose himself to as many ideas as possible, and hope that the same one would catch his attention as must have caught Netlord's.

And when the answer did strike him, it was so far-fetched and monstrous that he could not believe he was on the right track. He thought it would make an interesting plot for a story, but he could not accept it for himself. He felt an exasperating lack of accomplishment when the library closed for the day and he had to drive back up again to Kenscoff.

He headed straight for the bar of the Châtelet des Fleurs and the long relaxing drink that he had looked forward to all the way up. The waiter who was on duty brought him a note with it.

Dear Mr Templar,

I'm sorry your visit yesterday had to be so short. If it wouldn't bore you too much, I should enjoy another meeting. Could you come to dinner tonight? Just send word by the bearer.

Sincerely,
Theron Netlord

175

Simon glanced up.

"Is someone still waiting for an answer?"

"Yes, sir. Outside."

The Saint pulled out his pen and scribbled at the foot of the note:

Thanks. I'll be with you about 7.

S.T.

He decided, practically in the same instant in which the irresponsible impulse occurred to him, against signing himself with the little haloed stick figure which he had made famous. As he handed the note back to the waiter he reflected that, in the circumstances, his mere acceptance was bravado enough.

4

THERE WERE drums beating somewhere in the hills, faint and far-off, calling and answering each other from different directions, their sound wandering and echoing through the night so that it was impossible ever to be certain just where a particular tattoo had come from. It reached inside Netlord's house as a kind of vague vibration, like the endless thin chorus of nocturnal insects, which was so persistent that the ear learned to filter it out and for long stretches would be quite deaf to it, and then, in a lull in the conversation, with an infinitesimal re-tuning of attention, it would come back in a startling crescendo.

Theron Netlord caught the Saint listening at one of those moments, and said: "They're having a *bruler zin* tonight."

"What's that?"

"The big voodoo festive ceremony which climaxes most of the special rites. Dancing, litanies, invocation, possession by *loas*, more dances, sacrifice, more invocations and possessions, more dancing. It won't begin until much later. Right now they're just telling each other about it, warming up and getting in the mood."

Simon had been there for more than an hour, and this was the first time there had been any mention of voodoo.

Netlord had made himself a good if somewhat overpowering host. He mixed excellent rum cocktails, but without offering his guest the choice of anything else. He made stimulating conversation, salted with recurrent gibes at bureaucratic government and the Welfare State, but he held the floor so energetically that it was almost impossible to take advantage of the provocative openings he offered.

Simon had not seen Sibao again. Netlord had opened the door himself, and the cocktail makings were already on a side table in the living-room. There had been subdued rustlings and clinkings behind a screen that almost closed a dark alcove at the far end of the room, but no servant announced dinner: presently Netlord had announced it himself, and led the way around the screen and switched on a light, revealing a damask-covered table set for two and burdened additionally with chafing-dishes, from which he himself served rice, asparagus, and a savoury chicken stew rather like *coq au vin*. It was during one of the dialogue breaks induced by eating that Netlord had caught Simon listening to the drums.

"*Bruler* – that means 'burn'," said the Saint. "But what is *zin*?"

"The *zin* is a special earthenware pot. It stands on a tripod, and a fire is lighted under it. The *mambo* kills a sacrificial chicken by sticking her finger down into its mouth and tearing its throat open." Netlord took a hearty mouthful of stew. "She sprinkles blood and feathers in various places, and the plucked hens go into the pot with some corn. There's a chant:

> *Hounsis là yo, levez, nous domi trope;*
> *Hounsis là yo, levez, pour nous laver yeux nous:*
> *Gadé qui l'heu li yé.*

Later on she serves the boiling food right into the bare hands of the *hounsis*. Sometimes they put their bare feet in the flames too. It doesn't hurt them. The pots are left on the fire till they get red hot and crack, and everyone shouts '*Zin yo craqués!*'"

"It sounds like a big moment," said the Saint gravely. "If I could understand half of it."

"You mean you didn't get very far with your researches today?"

Simon felt the involuntary contraction of his stomach muscles, but he was able to control his hands so that there was no check in the smooth flow of what he was doing.

"How did you know about my researches?" he asked, as if he were only amused to have them mentioned.

"I dropped in to see Atherton Lee this morning, and asked after you. He told me where you'd gone. He said he'd told you about my interest in voodoo, and he supposed you were getting primed for an argument. I must admit that encouraged me to hope you'd accept my invitation tonight."

The Saint thought that might well qualify among the great understatements of the decade, but he did not let himself show it. After their first reflex leap his pulses ran like cool clockwork.

"I didn't find out too much," he said, "except that voodoo is a lot more complicated than I imagined. I thought it was just a few primitive superstitions that the slaves brought with them from Africa."

"Of course, some of it came from Dahomey. But how did it get there? The voodoo story of the Creation ties up with the myths of ancient Egypt. The Basin of Damballah – that's a sort of font at the foot of a voodoo altar – is obviously related to the blood trough at the foot of a Mayan altar. Their magic uses the Pentacle – the same mystic figure that medieval European magicians believed in. If you know anything about it, you can find links with eighteenth-century Masonry in some of their rituals, and even the design of the *vêvers*—"

"Those are sacred drawings that are supposed to summon the gods to take possession of their devotees, aren't they? I read about them."

"Yes, when the *houngan* draws them by dripping ashes and corn meal from his fingers, with the proper invocation. And doesn't that remind you of the sacred sand paintings of the Navajos? Do you see how all those roots must go back to a common source that's older than any written history?"

Netlord stared at the Saint challengingly, in one of those rare pauses where he waited for an answer.

Simon's fingertips touched the hard shape of the little tin plaque that was still in his shirt pocket, but he decided against showing it, and again he checked the bet.

"I saw a drawing of the *vêver* of Erzulie in a book," he said. "Somehow, it made me think of Catholic symbols connected with the Virgin Mary – with the heart, the stars, and the 'M' over it."

"Why not? Voodoo is pantheistic. The Church is against voodoo, not voodoo against the Church. Part of the purification prescribed for anyone who's being initiated as a *hounsis-canzo* is to go to church and make confession. Jesus Christ and the Virgin Mary are regarded as powerful intermediaries to the highest gods. Part of the litany they'll chant tonight at the *bruler zin* goes: *Grâce, Marie, grâce, Marie grâce, grâce, Marie grâce, Jésus, pardonnez-nous!*"

"Seriously?"

"The invocation of Legbas Atibon calls on St Antony of Padua: *Par pouvoir St-Antoine de Padoue.* And take the invocation of my own patron, Ogoun Feraille. It begins: *Par pouvoir St-Jacques Majeur . . .*"

"Isn't that blasphemy?" said the Saint. "I mean, a kind of deliberate sacrilege, like they're supposed to use in a Black Mass, to win the favour of devils by defiling something holy?"

Netlord's fist crashed on the table like a thunderclap.

"No, it isn't! The truth can't be blasphemous. Sacrilege is sin invented by bigots to try to keep God under contract to their own exclusive club. As if supernatural facts could be altered by human name-calling! There are a hundred sects all claiming to be the only true Christianity, and Christianity is only one of thousands of religions, all claiming to have the only genuine divine revelation. But the real truth is bigger than any one of them and includes them all!"

"I'm sorry," said the Saint. "I forgot that you were a convert."

"Lee told you that, of course. I don't deny it." The metallic grey eyes probed the Saint like knives. "I suppose you think I'm crazy."

"I'd rather say I was puzzled."

"Because you wouldn't expect a man like me to have any time for mysticism."

"Maybe."

Netlord poured some more wine.

"That's where you show your own limitations. The whole trouble with Western civilization is that it's blind in one eye. It doesn't believe in anything that can't be weighed and measured or reduced to a mathematical or chemical formula. It thinks it knows all the answers because it invented airplanes and television and hydrogen bombs. It thinks other cultures were backward because they fooled around with levitation and telepathy and raising the dead instead of killing the living. Well, some mighty clever people were living in Asia and Africa and Central America, thousands of years before Europeans crawled out of their caves. What makes you so sure that they didn't discover things that you don't understand?"

"I'm not so sure, but—"

"Do you know why I got ahead of everybody else in business? Because I never wore a blinker over one eye. If anyone said he could do anything, I never said 'That's impossible.' I said 'Show me how.' I don't care who I learn from, a college professor or a ditch-digger, a Chinaman or a nigger – so long as I can use what he knows."

The Saint finished eating and picked up his glass.

"And you think you'll find something in voodoo that you can use?"

"I have found it. Do you know what it is?"

Simon waited to be told, but apparently it was not another of Netlord's rhetorical questions. But when it was clear that a reply was expected, he said: "Why should I?"

"That's what you were trying to find out at the Public Library."

"I suppose I can admit that," Simon said mildly. "I'm a seeker for knowledge, too."

"I was afraid you would be, Templar, as soon as I heard your name. Not knowing who you were, I'd talked a little too much last night. It wouldn't have mattered with anyone else, but as the Saint you'd be curious about me. You'd have to ask questions. Lee would tell you about my interest in voodoo. Then you'd try to find out what I could use voodoo for. I knew all that when I asked you to come here tonight."

"And I knew you knew all that when I accepted."

"Put your cards on the table, then. What did your reading tell you?"

Simon felt unwontedly stupid. Perhaps because he had let Netlord do most of the talking, he must have done more than his own share of eating and drinking. Now it was an effort to keep up the verbal swordplay.

"It wasn't too much help," he said. "The mythology of voodoo was quite fascinating, but I couldn't see a guy like you getting a large charge out of spiritual trimmings. You'd want something that meant power, or money, or both. And the books I got hold of today didn't have much factual material about the darker side of voodoo – the angles that I've seen played up in lurid fiction."

"Don't stop now."

The Saint felt as if he lifted a slender blade once more against a remorseless bludgeon.

"Of course," he said, and meant to say it lightly, "you might really have union and government trouble if it got out that Netlord Underwear was being made by American zombies."

"So you guessed it," Netlord said.

5

SIMON TEMPLAR stared.
He had a sensation of utter unreality, as if at some point he had slipped from wakeful life into a nightmare without being aware of the moment when he fell asleep. A separate part of his brain seemed to hear his own voice at a distance.

"You really believe in zombies?"

"That isn't a matter of belief. I've seen them. A zombie prepared and served this dinner. That's why he was ordered not to let you see him."

"Now I really need the cliché: this I have got to see!"

"I'm afraid he's left for the night," Netlord said matter-of-factly.

"But you know how to make 'em?"

"Not yet. He belongs to the *houngan*. But I shall know before the sun comes up tomorrow. In a little while I shall go down to the *houmfort*, and the *houngan* will admit me to the last mysteries. The *bruler zin* afterwards is to celebrate that."

"Congratulations. What did you have to do to rate this?"

"I've promised to marry his daughter, Sibao."

Simon felt as if he had passed beyond the capacity for surprise. A soft blanket of cotton wool was folding around his mind. Yet the other part of him kept talking.

"Do you mean that?"

"Don't be absurd. As soon as I know all I need to, I can do without both of them."

"But suppose they resent that."

"Let me tell you something. Voodoo is a very practical kind of insurance. When a member is properly initiated, certain parts of a sacrifice and certain things from his body go into a little urn called the *pot de tête*, and after that the vulnerable element of his soul stays in the urn, which stays in the *houmfort*."

"Just like a safe deposit."

"And so, no one can lay an evil spell on him."

"Unless they can get hold of his *pot de tête*."

"So you see how easily I can destroy them if I act first."

The Saint moved his head as if to shake and clear it. It was like trying to shake a ton weight.

"It's very good of you to tell me all this," he articulated mechanically. "But what makes you so confidential?"

"I had to know how you'd respond to my idea when you knew it. Now you must tell me, truthfully."

"I think it stinks."

"Suppose you knew that I had creatures working for me, in a factory – zombies, who'd give me back all the money they'd nominally have to earn, except the bare minimum required for food and lodging. What would you do?"

"Report it to some authority that could stop you."

"That mightn't be so easy. A court that didn't believe in zombies couldn't stop people voluntarily giving me money."

"In that case," Simon answered deliberately, "I might just have to kill you."

Netlord sighed heavily.

"I expected that too," he said. "I only wanted to be sure. That's why I took steps in advance to be able to control you."

The Saint had known it for some indefinite time. He was conscious of his body sitting in a chair, but it did not seem to belong to him.

"You bastard," he said. "So you managed to feed me some kind of dope. But you're really crazy if you think that'll help you."

Theron Netlord put a hand in his coat pocket and took out a small automatic. He levelled it at the Saint's chest, resting his forearm on the table.

"It's very simple," he said calmly. "I could kill you now, and easily account for your disappearance. But I like the idea of having you work for me. As a zombie, you could retain many of your unusual abilities. So I could kill you, and, after I've learned a little more tonight, restore you to living death. But that would impair your usefulness in certain ways. So I'd rather apply what I know already, if I can, and make you my creature without harming you physically."

"That's certainly considerate of you," Simon scoffed.

He didn't know what unquenchable spark of defiance gave him the will to keep up the hopeless bluff. He seemed to have no contact with any muscles below his neck. But as long as he didn't try to move, and fail, Netlord couldn't be sure of that.

"The drug is only to relax you," Netlord said. "Now look at this."

He dipped his left hand in the ashtray beside him, and quickly began drawing a pattern with his fingertips on the white tablecloth – a design of crisscross diagonal lines with other vertical lines rising through the diamonds they formed, the verticals tipped with stars and curlicues, more than anything like the picture of an ornate wrought-iron gate. And as he drew it he intoned in a strange chanting voice:

"*Par pouvoir St-Jacques Majeur, Ogoun Badagris nèg Baguidi, Bago, Ogoun Feraille nèg fer, nèg feraille, nèg tagnifer nago, Ogoun batala, nèg, nèg Ossagne malor, Ossangne aquiquan, Ossangne agouelingui, Jupiter tonnerre, nèg blabla, nèg oloncoun, nèg vante-m pas fie'm. . . . Aocher nago, aocher nago, aocher nago!*"

The voice had risen, ending on a kind of muted shout, and there was a blaze of fanatic excitement and something weirder than that in Netlord's dilated eyes.

Simon wanted to laugh. He said: "What's that – a sequel to the Hutsut Song?" Or he said: "I prefer '*Twas brillig and the slithy toves*'." Or perhaps he said neither, for the thoughts and the ludicrousness and the laugh were suddenly chilled and empty, and it was like a hollowness and a darkness, like stepping into nothingness and a quicksand opening under his feet, sucking him down, only it was the mind that went down, the lines of the wrought-iron gate pattern shimmering and blinding before his eyes, and a black horror such as he had never known rising around him. . . .

Out of some untouched reserve of willpower he wrung the strength to clear his vision again for a moment, and to shape words that he knew came out, even though they came through stiff clumsy lips.

"Then I'll have to kill you right now," he said.

He tried to get up. He had to try now. He couldn't pretend any longer that he was immobile from choice. His limbs felt like lead. His body was encased in invisible concrete. The triumphant fascinated face of Theron Netlord blurred in his sight.

The commands of his brain went out along nerves that swallowed them in enveloping numbness. His mind was drowning in the swelling dreadful dark. He thought: "Sibao, your Maitresse Erzulie must be the weak sister in this league."

And suddenly he moved.

As if taut wires had snapped, he moved. He was on his feet. Uncertainly, like a thawing out, like a painful return of circulation, he felt connections with his body linking up again. He saw the exultation in Netlord's face crumple into rage and incredulous terror.

"Fooled you, didn't I?" said the Saint croakily. "You must still need some coaching on your hex technique."

Netlord moved his hand a little, rather carefully, and his knuckle whitened on the trigger of the automatic. The range was point-blank.

Simon's eardrums rang with the shot, and something struck him a stunning blinding blow over the heart. He had an impression of being hurled backwards as if by the blow of a giant fist; and then with no recollection of falling he knew that he was lying on the floor, half under the table, and he had no strength to move any more.

6

THERON NETLORD rose from his chair and looked down, shaken by the pounding of his own heart. He had done many brutal things in his life, but he had never killed anyone before. It had been surprisingly easy to do, and he had been quite deliberate about it. It was only afterwards that the shock shook him, with his first understanding of the new loneliness into which he had irrevocably stepped, the apartness from all other men that only murderers know.

Then a whisper and a stir of movement caught his eye and ear together, and he turned his head and saw Sibao. She wore the white dress and the white handkerchief on her head, and the necklaces of threaded seeds and grain, that were prescribed for what was to be done that night.

"What are you doing here?" he snarled in Creole. "I said I would meet you at the *houmfort*."

"I felt there was need for me."

She knelt by the Saint, touching him with her sensitive hands. Netlord put the gun in his pocket and turned to the sideboard. He uncorked a bottle of rum, poured some into a glass, and drank.

Sibao stood before him again.

"Why did you want to kill him?"

"He was – he was a bad man. A thief."

"He was good."

"No, he was clever." Netlord had had no time to prepare for questions. He was improvising wildly, aware of the hollowness of his invention and trying to bolster it with truculence. "He must have been waiting for a chance to meet you. If that had not happened, he would have found another way. He came to rob me."

"What could he steal?"

Netlord pulled out his wallet, and took from it a thick pad of currency. He showed it to her.

"He knew that I had this. He would have killed me for it." There were twenty-five crisp hundred-dollar bills, an incredible fortune by the standards of a Haitian peasant, but only the amount of pocket money that Netlord normally carried and would have felt undressed without. The girl's dark velvet eyes rested on it, and he was quick to see more possibilities. "It was a present I was going to give to you and your father tonight." Money was the strongest argument he had ever known. He went on with newfound confidence: "Here, take it now."

She held the money submissively.

"But what about – him?"

"We must not risk trouble with the police. Later we will take care of him, in our own way. . . . But we must go now, or we shall be late."

He took her compellingly by the arm, but for a moment she still held back.

"You know that when you enter the *sobagui* to be cleansed, your *loa*, who sees all things, will know if there is any untruth in your heart."

"I have nothing to fear." He was sure of it now. There was nothing in voodoo that scared him. It was simply a craft that he had set out to master, as he had mastered everything else that he made up his mind to. He would use it on others, but it could do nothing to him. "Come along, they are waiting for us."

Simon heard their voices before the last extinguishing wave of darkness rolled over him.

7

HE WOKE up with a start, feeling cramped and bruised from lying on the floor. Memory came back to him in full flood as he sat up. He looked down at his shirt. There was a black-rimmed hole in it, and even a grey scorch of powder around that. But when he examined his chest, there was no hole and no blood, only a pronounced soreness over the ribs. From his breast pocket he drew out the metal plaque with the *vêver* of Erzulie. The bullet had scarred and bent it, but it had struck at an angle and glanced off without even scratching him, tearing another hole in the shirt under his arm.

The Saint gazed at the twisted piece of tin with an uncanny tingle feathering his spine.

Sibao must have known he was unhurt when she touched him. Yet she seemed to have kept the knowledge to herself. Why?

He hoisted himself experimentally to his feet. He knew that he had first been drugged, then over that lowered resistance almost completely mesmerized; coming on top of that, the deadened impact of the bullet must have knocked him out, as a punch over the heart could knock out an already groggy boxer. But now all the effects seemed to have worn off together, leaving only a tender spot on his chest and an insignificant muzziness in his head. By his watch, he had been out for about two hours.

The house was full of the silence of emptiness. He went through a door to the kitchen, ran some water, and bathed his face. The only other sound there was the ticking of a cheap clock.

Netlord had said that only the two of them were in the house. And Netlord had gone – with Sibao.

Gone to something that everything in the Saint's philosophy

must refuse to believe. But things had happened to himself already that night which he could only think of incredulously. And incredulity would not alter them, or make them less true.

He went back through the living-room and out on to the front veranda. Ridge beyond ridge, the mysterious hills fell away from before him under a full yellow moon that dimmed the stars; and there was no jeep in the driveway at his feet.

The drums still pulsed through the night, but they were no longer scattered. They were gathered together, blending in unison and counterpoint, but the acoustical tricks of the mountains still masked their location. Their muttering swelled and receded with chance shifts of air, and the echoes of it came from all around the horizon, so that the whole world seemed to throb softly with it.

There was plenty of light for him to walk down to the Châtelet des Fleurs.

He found Atherton Lee and the waiter starting to put out the lights in the bar. The innkeeper looked at him in a rather startled way.

"Why – what happened?" Lee asked.

Simon sat up at the counter and lighted a cigarette.

"Pour me a Barbancourt," he said defensively, "and tell me why you think anything happened."

"Netlord brought the jeep back. He told me he'd taken you to the airport – you'd had some news which made you suddenly decide to catch the night plane to Miami, and you just had time to make it. He was coming back tomorrow to pick up your things and send them after you."

"Oh, that," said the Saint blandly. "When the plane came through, it turned out to have filled up at Cuidad Trujillo. I couldn't get on. So I changed my mind again. I ran into some-one downtown who gave me a lift back."

He couldn't say: "Netlord thought he'd just murdered me, and he was laying the foundation for me to disappear without being missed." Somehow, it sounded so ridiculous, even with a bullet hole in his shirt. And if he were pressed for details, he would have to say: "He was trying to put some kind of hex on me, or make me a zombie." That would be assured of a great reception. And then the police would have to be brought in. Perhaps Haiti was the only country on earth where a policeman might feel obliged to listen seriously to such a story; but the police were still the police. And just at those times when most people automatically turn to the police, Simon Templar's instinct was to avoid them.

What would have to be settled now between him and Theron Netlord he would settle himself, in his own way.

The waiter, closing windows and emptying ashtrays, was singing to himself under his breath:

> "*Moin pralé nan Sibao,*
> *Chaché, chaché, loléo—*"

"What's that?" Simon asked sharply.

"Just Haitian song, sir."

"What does it mean?"

"It mean, *I will go to Sibao* – that holy place in voodoo, sir. *I take oil for lamp*, it say. *If you eat food of Legba you will have to die:*

> "*Si ou mangé mangé Legba,*
> *Ti ga çon onà mouri, oui.*
> *Moin pralé nan Sibao—*"

"After spending on evening with Netlord, you should know all about that," Atherton Lee said.

Simon downed his drink and stretched out a yawn.

"You're right. I've had enough of it for one night," he said. "I'd better let you go on closing up – I'm ready to hit the sack myself."

But he lay awake for a long time, stretched out on his bed in the moonlight. Was Theron Netlord merely insane, or was there even the most fantastic possibility that he might be able to make use of things that modern materialistic science did not understand? Would it work on Americans, in America? Simon remembered that one of the books he had read referred to a certain American evangelist as *un houngan insuffisamment instruit*; and it was a known fact that that man controlled property worth millions, and that his followers turned over all their earnings to him, for which he gave them only food, shelter and sermons. Such things *had* happened, and were as unsatisfactory to explain away as flying saucers. . . .

The ceaseless mutter of the distant drums mocked him till he fell asleep.

Si ou mangé mangé Legba
Ti ga çon onà mouri, oui!

He awoke and still heard the song. The moonlight had given way to the grey light of dawn, and the first thing he was conscious of was a fragile unfamiliar stillness left void because the drums were at last silent. But the voice went on – a flat, lifeless, distorted voice that was nevertheless recognizable in a way that sent icy filaments crawling over his scalp.

Moin pralé nan Sibao,
Moin pralé nan Sibao,
Moin pralé nan Sibao,
Chaché, chaché, lolé-o . . .

His window overlooked the road that curved up past the inn, and he was there while the song still drifted up to it. The two of them stood directly beneath him – Netlord, and the slender black girl dressed all in white. The girl looked up and saw Simon, as if she had expected to. She raised one hand and solemnly made a pattern in the air, a shape that somehow blended the outlines of a heart and an ornate letter M, quickly and intricately, and her lips moved with it: it was curiously like a benediction.

Then she turned to the man beside her, as she might have turned to a child.

"*Venez,*" she said.

The tycoon also looked up, before he obediently followed her. But there was no recognition, no expression at all, in the grey face that had once been so ruthless and domineering; and all at once Simon knew why Theron Netlord would be no problem to him or to anyone, any more.